I0658472

LETTERS

JOHN COLLINS

LET'S RETHINK THAT
Atlanta, GA
www.letsrethinkthat.com

DEDICATION

Byron.

You were a giant among insects, man. The impact you made on our lives will forever be etched on our hearts as we release your physical presence to our God in Heaven. Rest in Paradise. I love you, young'un, and will miss your squeaky voice, benevolent smile, your sarcasm, your chuckle, and the amazing treasures given from your heart to those much closer to you. Keep an eye out for us here on Earth.

CONTENTS

CPR

Hope. I was *counting* on it! I *demanded* he hold on! I told his arrogant ass to man the hell up and be the tough guy he always is! I could *feel* him...he was trying. I could feel him trying to stay with me! I watched helplessly as everything started crossing my mind going from confusion to reality.

Time was ticking loudly from the oversized clock hanging above my bed. Everything was amplified as the adrenalin bombarding its way through my veins had a morphine effect on my emotions. A sudden weight. I could feel all of his weight on me in an unusual way. It was...sudden. There was nothing in him to manipulate his body. I didn't want to accept the fact that he was...maybe.

NO! I recited a myriad of CPR skills to myself preparing to resuscitate someone I knew intimately. This was not a training scenario. This was the real thing! I was soaking in his blood as I flipped his body off me with quick cautious care. I focused on being his first responder and his life support system. I was trying to keep from going into shock as the dog started barking hysterically next to my leg.

An autonomous blueprint unfolded in my mind reminding me that I needed to do a scene size up and body assessment. I tuned the sounds of Batman's barking out with muted awareness. I was nervous. Everything went wrong so fast and for the wrong reasons and here I was in the middle of a love triangle I created unwittingly! The man responsible for this crime scene was one of my...closest... homeboys. Wait! How? It was at that point I tuned into his muttering as he paced across the wooden floor like a lunatic. It wasn't Gary holding the gun.

Gary had just been shot, jumping to protect me from Darius of all people. He reached down to slowly pick up the weapon he dropped. I quickly grabbed the string to the lamp switching it on as it crashed to the floor. It rocked back and forth on its broken shell shining light dimly against the wall. Darius began a steady pace muttering to himself in a rapid rhythm. His shadow passed over me with indecisive chaos. The curtain covering the open window parted making way for the calm night air to flow into my bedroom like it were observing the situation. I froze looking at him, trying to determine if he was a threat to me. I studied him, holding my breath, watching him behave like I had never seen him carry on before.

The training from my Navy Corpsmen days kicked in, and my first instinct was to protect my patient. I counted his paces for a couple of turns, committing the sound of each step to memory on that section of the floor to gauge his distance. I noticed he wasn't looking at me, nor was he focused on any one thing. I looked down at my red stained arms and bare chest. The blood felt cold and damp against my skin, clutching onto my abdomen like Gary did when we slept at night. The contents of an envelope that started an argument lay scattered across his pooling blood. Time seemed to be rotating within itself as if I was moving in slow motion, but everything around me was on its normal course.

When I looked at Gary's face, I realized I was wasting much of that time. I looked at the three holes burrowed through his chest and started praying to myself. I didn't care about my own safety at that point. I gave two rescue breaths and reached for my phone. I quickly pushed the button for Emergency and sat the phone on the floor hitting the speaker button. I listened for the operator and tuned in to make sure Darius' pattern had not strayed.

"9-1-1, what is your emergency?" The operator stated. She sounded like she had an attitude, which woke up the Detroit in me. I kept pumping Gary's chest, as I yelled into the phone with a quick glare.

"Umm, girl! My boyfriend has been shot! And I need the police and an ambulance over here, please! This ain't the hood! My name is Jason Williams!" I said quickly wiping my hands on the bed to dry them as much as I could. I was starting to sweat.

"Yes sir, to whom am I speaking?" she asked, still giving me just a little too much on this *emergency* phone call.

CPR

"Jason! Williams!" I yelled, knowing full hell well I told this *shady* heffa my name already. I rattled off my address.

"Mr. Williams, I have a lock on your location."

"Good to go!" I said.

"I am dispatching units to your residence as we speak. Is the attacker still in the domicile with you, sir?" The operator responded suddenly with a corrected tone. I looked up and saw Darius still pacing and talking to himself. He looked over at me with a squint and paused. I kept pumping Gary's chest as our eyes locked. The operator repeated her question. I tilted Gary's head back and administered two breaths and returned to pumping his chest. I then looked up at Darius while counting the chest compressions in my head.

"Yes, ma'am, he is. I'm looking at him right now," I answered as I checked to see if Gary had any signs of life. Batman trotted over to Gary's foot and began whimpering and licking his toes doing his part to help. Batman had done this many times before when it was time for Gary to wake up for work. Gary would joke and say, *"That's da lil' rat dogs smart ass way of kicking me outta yur house, babes. Little mutt..."* Batman would always fight for my attention when Gary was around.

"Sir, are you able to get away from the attacker?" the operator asked.

"MISS! I'm doing CPR on my partner. NO! Just send me some help! I need...some help," I said frantically wondering why my efforts weren't reviving him. *AND!* I wondered why I had to keep getting this girl *TOGETHER?! REALLY, FISH?!* I gave Gary two more breaths and checked for a pulse to see if he was breathing on his own. His body remained limp as the blood drained from his wounds. I stayed strong, trying not to freak out, praying, fighting for my dude's life, keeping an eye out on psycho, and listening out for a freakin' siren! I was trying to figure out how to stop the bleeding. I thought to myself, *Blood carries oxygen throughout the body. He's losing blood dummy!* I also kept telling myself to hold it together over and over.

"Okay, sir, I understand your dilemma, but you also have to think about your safety as well. What is your attacker doing? Is he armed?" she asked. I grabbed my first aid bag from under the bed, unzipping it.

"He is, he is just pacing right now," I said as Darius lost it when the sounds of sirens finally became audible.

"FUCK! THINK! THINK! THINK! THINK!" he yelled, slapping his head with his palms. He reached down to pick up the gun. I applied a pressure dressing to Gary's wounds as the flashing lights made their way in through the window upstairs.

"Sir, are you still there?" the operator asked. I gave two more breaths relieved that help had arrived.

"Yes, ma'am!" I said taking a second to catch my breath. "The cops or hopefully an ambulance is outside!"

CPR

I heard a loud banging on the front door. Batman started barking and ran from under Gary's foot past Darius. I continued doing CPR watching Darius with one eye.

"What the fuck did I just do? What did I just do?! NO! Wait it...it, it, it was self-defense. No, I can't say that bullshit, I'm black!" he said rationalizing aloud. "Yeah, yeah, yeah, I lost my...yeah...naw, THINK!" Darius stated as the sound of footsteps up the stairs became apparent. "FUCK!" He tapped the barrel of the gun against his temple. "That nigga was no good, he...he dogged my boy out. JASON! HE DOGGED YOU OUT, MY DUDE! And you SAVING HIS PUNK ASS?!" He stopped pacing and turned in my direction. "I did CPR once! Mmm hmmph, SEE! You ain't know that shit about your boy Dee, huh?" He said tapping the gun to his chest offering a cocky smirk for a smile. His face contorted as he pointed the gun to his head. "Uh huh, that shit don't work! MMM MMM!! IT don't WORK! It don't work! JASON! IT DON'T work!" He started sweating and wiped his forehead with his shirtsleeve pointing the gun in Gary's general direction. "It didn't revive Mendez and it damn sure won't revive that disgusting ass Rasta nigga, either! Don't you see it ain't working for this muthafucka?! Fuck him. Listen to ME! GAD'DAMMIT!"

I stopped what I was doing when he pointed the gun at me and cocked it back gritting his teeth. He took a quick dab at the drool leaking from his lips with the back of his free hand. The angle he was holding the pistol suggested to me he was aiming for my forehead. We were both great shooters in the Navy with Darius being one of the few Corpsman in our bunch to damn near shoot close to sniper level. I'm exaggerating, but he handles a firearm quite well. It was his way of getting in touch with what he liked to call his inner hood nigga.

"Darius. Chill. Please, chill, alright?" I asked in a calm manner. I raised my blood-drenched hands and gave him my full attention. I knew that I would be okay, but I suspected that Darius wouldn't be the same again for a while though. "It's going to be okay," I said trying to believe that statement my damn self.

"Mr. Williams, the police are there and should be entering your residence to assist you. Okay?" the operator asked. I nodded my head yes like she was sitting in front of me. I forgot her phony ass was on the phone, pro'ly eatin' popcorn or some junk. Darius was stone faced. He looked down scanning Gary's body. He took a shot at the phone causing me to jump as the pieces ricocheted off the wall. One piece grazed my shoulder.

"So, I gotta lose you too, huh? My soldiers, my baby girl, my chance of a normal fucking marriage." He rubbed his face and gritted his teeth looking like he was holding back tears. "My chance of an un-fucked up life with you...maybe! You did this shit to me! So, I did this shit FOR YOU! For love. You couldn't wait for me? HUH? I told you

I was trying to figure this shit out for you and me. You couldn't wait for me, JASON?! ANSWER ME! RIGHT NOW! Answer...me," he demanded with a hard swallow and a serious glare. He assumed his original stance pointing the gun at me. Finger finessing the trigger.

"Darius, I've always been by your side, but listen to me! We gotta get Gary some help, Dee. I hear you. I do, LT. We're Corpsmen first and we gotta job to do, okay," I pleaded with a stern voice. I was scared as shit, but I couldn't let him see that. "Let's get this man some help. All right...? Help me out, shipmate." I saw a white police officer slowly creeping into view through my peripheral. I made no sudden eye movement. I didn't want to tip Darius off and I hoped to GOD the cop didn't shoot *both* our black asses.

"I'm confused, Jason! Cause, THAT NIGGA DEAD! And from my vantage point, you over there on his side, not mine! Rasta mon' not me, shipmate," he said defiantly. "What was ya'll fighting about?"

"Darius, man, he needs help!" I scoffed.

"SHUT UP! What was ya'll arguing about? Me?! Huh?!"

"That's not impor..."

"You know what the fuck I went through for this, this, this...this thing with you and me not to work the fuck out? Yeah, THAT NIGGA DEAD! FUCK! I killed him! I mean...I ain't mean to, Jason. I ain't mean to do it! I mean... This wasn't...YO! LOOK AT ME!" he screamed as I quickly took my eyes off Gary's body to catch Darius' glare. "HE DEAD! SEE, WATCH! He can't hurt you no more." He stepped forward, pulled the trigger, and unloaded a round into Gary's body. I flinched at the sight of a quarter sized rupture appearing in Gary's shoulder from the displacement of the bullet. Blood spatter misted my face. "SO, WHAT'S UP?! HUH?!

I watched a gun aimed at me fall to the floor as his body stiffened like a dart. I saw the whites of his eyes bulge as he let out a deep growl that sounded like someone had their hands wrapped tightly around his throat. He toppled to the floor with a solid thud. The police officer released the trigger on his taser and straddled Darius, strong-arming him onto his stomach, pinning him to the floor.

Darius took a deep audible breath coming to a relaxed state. The cop placed him in a set of cuffs reciting the Miranda Rights as Darius took in another huge audible gulp of air. The second officer yelled an ALL CLEAR, asking if I was okay, as he moved in to remove me from the scene. I didn't say anything. On the way out of the room, he told me his name was Officer Anderson. The EMTs rushed in to assist with Gary. The officer walked me down the stairs and outside to his police cruiser. Batman was hot on my heels. I reached down and scooped him up half way down.

CPR

The cop opened the trunk and put on a pair of gloves. He pulled out a thin wool blanket from a plastic wrapper then handed me a towel and some wet wipes to clean up with. He told me to just place everything in a red plastic bag he sat on the trunk. I wiped my arms, hands, face and Batman down also. I took the blanket and wrapped it around myself as he opened the front door and offered me a seat. I got into the car. He asked if I was okay. I didn't respond. He told me he'd get a statement from me shortly and closed the door. I watched the EMT's wheel an empty stretcher out of the house. That could only mean one thing. My heart felt muzzled. I had an urge to throw up as the smell of blood triggered my senses.

I watched the stretcher slowly pass by with a medical bag serving as its only passenger. Batman peeked out of the window and then up at me and started to lick my face as I tried to process how to tell Gary's parents what had just happened. I hadn't fully grasped the concept of what just happened, yet. I realized I didn't have my phone. I looked around and noticed some of my neighbors gathered across the street. I couldn't begin to articulate how this all felt.

This was some ol' Lifetime TV drama type of mess. I don't do this! Homicide, on the 7 o'clock news tease! I could imagine the headline. How in the world can I describe this to Mama Larrieux? She just lost her eldest boy on my watch. This time I had to be dreaming. I had to be fast asleep in my bed. But gravity had its way with my stomach when reality started yelling.

"I'm sorry, Jason! I'M SORRY! I'm sorry! I'm sorry!" Darius kept yelling this sentiment as the officer manhandled him all the way to the second police cruiser. It was as if he was asking me to do something to help him out of the cuffs. I could feel him pleading for my help. The cop wrangled him through the door making sure he was seated properly. I've seen black men arrested on the news for crimes all the time. I even felt like many of them were innocent. We see it so much you become immune to it doing all you can to hope it won't be you. We always want to give our brothas the benefit of the doubt. Now to see Darius with my own eyes, in this predicament, blatantly guilty, crushed me. Crushed me.

I looked down at Batman, who was looking at me with soulful eyes. He was shaking pressed thankfully against me. I began petting his damp silky coat trying to decide which emotion was appropriate to use first. I had lost one of my closest friends and my partner like a set of keys. Do I not deserve a happily ever after? I tossed Batman to the side and quickly opened the car door to leave all the contents of my stomach on the pavement. I took a few deep breaths wiping my mouth and spit before closing the door. I rested my head on the headrest.

What's left in "us" to stray when love gets in the way? I couldn't possibly cry tonight...

PTSD

"So, are you going to open up in today's session, Lieutenant Westbrook?" That was becoming a routine question for the psychologist the Navy assigned to me. It became his form of a pleasant hello. I wasn't ready to say shit. I looked out of the window, leaning back in the chair debating on a couple of cocky answer choices. I didn't want to say nothing at all because he said some shit about PTSD. I ain't never feared four letters...well, love. With Jason, but PTSD is damn, that give these military doctors the right to fuck with my head and then send my black ass to the VA as another number to collect some check for the rest of my life. I'm better than that.

I sat there thinking about random things. My orange jump suit glowed brighter than the light coming in from outside. The bars over the window reminded me that I was still on lock down at a United States military prison, better known as the brig to Navy service members. The coolness of the chains binding my hands and feet together correlated well with the chains I had mentally strapped myself securely into. *These nigga's ain't getting my damn mind. Fuck that.*

I looked at Commander Jamison who was smiling at me like he had always done. It was this phony ass sweet smile. Maybe that's how this fool smiles, I'ought know. I just wasn't feelin' the smug look on his face. He was a fit man, beginning his fifties, with the occasional squared away uniform. At least today his ass was. On paper he probably looked to be a slam-dunk for Captain with all the impressive chest candy to include a Sea Surface Warfare pin. One of them true wanna be military PhD types. He had awards and degrees, and Bravo Zulu's, Hail and Farewell plaques plastered all over the god damn place. His cockiness struck a chord with me. It reminded me of my dad when he talked to white people. He even sounded like him, like the way he annunciated every fucking letter and syllable in every word he spoke. You know, that English with no flavor added to it. Sterile and sharp like a #10 blade. It irritated me the last few times, and I couldn't remember why. But now I do. *Jason was always my go to person with my emotional shit.* Not this clown.

So, I stayed cool. I sat back. I listened. I calculated. I studied him and determined that after nine sessions of silence I could trust him. He was a brotha. I'm supposed to be able to trust the brothas in this field. But he's a *brother.* Since black people don't seek therapy and all. He claims he don't know my dad, although I find that hard to believe. I know the two of them have crossed paths. *Lying ass, nigga.* That was the first question out my mouth to him. And he says he don't know him though. I felt he was lying, but then you know maybe it would be like a conflict of interest or something if he took my case. The black officer community is tight knit. We gotta be, that's why I know he lyin'.

Naw, I can't trust this mu'fucka. *I ain't sayin' shit*, I thought as I studied the picture on his desk of his baby girl wearing a straw hat with bunny ears. She was sitting on the Easter Bunny's lap. Her dress was all frilly white with pink satin ribbons around the waist and on the Easter basket she was holding. I tried to frame a photo from my mind of how my daughter's face would look in that expensive frame. She would have been so beautiful, and I know I would be so proud. I had to catch myself from reaching out to grab the picture when the light reflected off the cuffs from my sudden movement...

"I had a little girl...once," I said quietly. I was so focused on the photo that I didn't realize I opened my mouth to speak. Normally, I'd be sitting in this same spot, staring out the window while he used this time to catch up on patient charts. The window gave me something to look forward to. This was the first time the picture was turned to where I could see her though. She was a beautiful cinnamon girl. Long curly hair that reminded me of my sister Lauren's.

"Is that what you wish to discuss today, Lieutenant?" CDR Jamison asked. He turned from staring at his computer monitor and ceased typing. I was put off by the way he addressed me. I clinched my teeth and closed my eyes regaining direct eye contact with him. That's how I knew he knew my dad. Brig inmates are stripped of rank. So, I know it was him respecting my dad to a degree. Not just officer to officer courtesy. I decided to test his motive via military bearing.

"With all due respect, Commander. I don't deserve that title anymore, sir. I pissed that away a year ago. Can you just use my last name, sir? Just for the record, I don't know who LT Westbrook is anymore..." I stated holding his gaze to let him know I meant business. *You ain't getting no favors, nigga'!* I clinched my fist and jumped when his phone rang. That's when I noticed my beard was dry and itching. I had to get some more of that lotion soon. A replay of Jason's smile came to mind. That shit was something I missed.

"Excuse me, let me turn this off. I do apologize. Very well. Westbrook. That will be fine. What's on your mind this morning? Remember nothing is off limits, you are not being recorded, and you are protected under HIPAA Privacy laws," doc said. I thought about how Jason used to always pack my favorite moisturizer in every care package he sent me on deployment. I would go through that shit like a fat rat. I don't know how much baby boy spent on all them boxes, but I appreciated it so much when I was deployed. We wrote letters and shit to one another because the snail mail was more secure than email. I sure could use one right about now. Since I already opened my damn mouth, I figured I might as well try to vent. Put this guy on probation with my mind. He need to know I ain't crazy. *Run tell my dad that, shit.*

"I...I never shot a man before...I don't like how what that...how...I just don't like how that...felt," I said looking out of the window. "I...just wanted to scare them a little bit, but when I..." I stopped and looked at the clock. "How much time do I have today?"

"You have as much time as you'd like. You are my only case this afternoon. Take your time, Westbrook," he said keeping his eye contact with me. That's good. I respected that. I squared myself away so I could stop stammering.

"Losing for me isn't an option," I said looking at him hoping he'd understand. Shit I didn't understand. "I was good, until I saw...the first casualty at our Battalion Aid Station. We were just outside of Kuwait. We were supposed to be in a safe zone. NO zone is a safe zone out there, sir. You don't know who to trust. Your mind is going and your head is on swivel even when you sleep. It was a simple BAS, that's all. I helped build this thing. I had shaken hands with POTUS there. I had just let a few of my Marines know they'd be able to go home as soon as the Med-Evac arrived. One of them had a little girl named Ruby. He named her after his grandmother. I was all proud to tell him I had one on the way. He only had 11 more minutes bef..." I closed my eyes and took a moment to swallow and breathe. "Before the black bird would have landed."

"Take your time. If you need a break at any time during your session, that is your right, Westbrook," CDR explained. I nodded and kept going.

"That's what we called them. Black birds. It was routine. I'm logging results, checking heads and beds, and a fucking mortar round blasts through th..." I stopped as the image of beds, troops, and staff all were catapulted towards the side of the Medical General-Purpose Tent I stood in. It was like I was there all over again. I felt the ground shake and the flash of intense heat again. "I lied to that brotha. I went to a dark place. Then to get hit later in a convoy. I...sir...they vanished right in front of me. Three lives. Two men and one woman that I worked with, ate with, shared close quarters with, planned with, my team was always ready and...there I was trying to bring Mendez back from the dead. I didn't notice I was resuscitating a torso. I...lost..."

"Take your time. It's okay," CDR said.

"It was the first thing in my life that my cunning, my dad's money and influence, or one of my college degrees couldn't fix..." I paused and got my thoughts together. My palms were sweating. The doctor wrote a few notes down on a pad. I waited until he finished with his scribbling.

"Westbrook, you do understand that no matter how prepared you are for combat, there will be variables beyond your control that you may face?" CDR Jamison asked.

"Sir, quite frankly, I am aware of that textbook PhD approach to war, but until you've held a torso in your arms. She was still in uniform sir! It's all practice until you face the real thing. I had started resuscitating on instinct, and then I needed more space so I could access her injuries. When I pull on her...she separated from...sir have you ever held a dead body? Someone you knew?" I asked in a serious tone. I don't know why I felt the need to talk today. I guess not getting a response from Jason brought me to my knees. He was really the only person I could probably address stuff like this with.

"I can't say that I have," CDR Jamison stated. His face showed that he was offering compassion and not judging me. He was trying to figure me out.

I learned a lot about people being in a combat zone. I learned a lot about myself. You start to love and care about your shipmates and your Marines without knowing it. You see how they operate; you study behaviors and routines and develop your own so that you know, and they know if something is off. In the military that's just how you operate. Routine keeps you alive and out of harms way in combat zones. You must be in tune with your surroundings to move seamlessly in stealth at a moment's notice. You listen. I had trained with these guys. I met their families and hugged their kids. I traded MRE's with them. I remember joking with Mendez, the only female officer assigned with me to, slide one of the fingers of death

(MRE hotdogs) into my mouth. Stupid jokes to break the ice. I pinned medals on them, laughed, and prayed with them. I believed that we'd all make it home safely to those we loved. You proudly do your job knowing that you are a part of a machine bigger than yourself.

"I watched my friend Jason lose his...lose someone because I let anger and jealousy take over my mind. I lost it all when I saw him doing CPR on...Gary. I messed up and embarrassed my dad and tarnished our good name. I can't forgive myself for what I did." I looked back at the clock. Only a few minutes had passed.

"What did you do?" CDR Jamison asked?

"Wait a minute, doc! They all selfish! They call me selfish...and, and, and, and a player. But that's what you do as a man, right doc? I mean...that's what the black man is supposed to do? Strip'em and dick'em! I'm just sayin'," I said looking around the room, it seemed to be spinning out of control when I looked back and focused on CDR Jamison. I didn't know what I was talking about. He became my dad sitting across from me. I got pissed instantly. "I looked up to you, Pops! I did! I looked up to you, and I finally think I can trust you and you bring up Jason and *Uncle Richard in the same breath*? What the fuck am I supposed to do with another Cartier watch Pops! I can't get the time back stolen from my youth with him making me do shit...I didn't think little boys should do...I wanted a family so bad so that I could do shit right! I fucking hate you, but I love you cause you're my Dad!"

"Westbrook! Take a breath. I need you to pace yourself," CDR Jamison stated. I suddenly realized where I was. He wasn't my dad. I swallowed hard and looked behind me nervously. I felt hot and I was soaked with perspiration.

"I took a life that wasn't mine to take." I took a minute to adjust my wrists in the cuffs they had me in. They were irritating me now that my skin was damp and clammy. The sound they made irritated me. I refocused on what I was thinking to say. "For no reason other than I didn't want...to lose Jason too, okay! So, I broke into his house. I didn't know what I was going to do, sir. I thought I'd scare the shit out of him that was all I really wanted. I just wanted to threaten him so that he wouldn't hurt Jason anymore. I couldn't stop the shit that happened in the desert, but I could fix this. I could set shit right. He didn't deserve someone like him...I...I got my gun...I loaded it in the car. I was trying to do it at the red lights. I had all these bullets on the floor," I swallowed and wiped the corners of my mouth reminded of the cuffs irritating rattle. "He left the garage door open. That's how I got in. I walked up the stairs and heard the two of them fighting. They were both yelling at each other back and forth." I felt myself getting upset so I took a breath, so I wouldn't lose it again.

"Are you okay?" he asked.

"I was trying to figure out what I was doing there. I kept asking myself, why the fuck was I there. And I kept getting more and more jealous staring and thinking about the good times Jason and me had." I looked out of the window then back at doc. I was failing at holding back tears.

"Are you okay, Westbrook?" CDR Jamison asked again. We can take a break if you need too.

"Sir, he wanted to lay in the arms of a rapist. My HOMEBOY! My dude! He...he...just abandoned ship with me because I missed what, a couple of phone calls of his? He let this dude get away with it and just tossed me aside. And I know what rape is, and I'm looking at this fool, and I'm looking at my gun, and I'm looking at the door, and I'm looking at my gun, and I'm looking at this fool. There was music playing and his dog was barking. And I'm processing all of this, standing there..." I took a moment to chill. "Catching a glimpse at Jason passionately defend himself. I took the safety off, lined up my sights, and entered the doorway. Jason looked like he stopped breathing when he saw me there with the gun, and I can honestly say I was aiming at him. I don't understand why." I looked out at the window again.

"Was there a struggle between you and your friend Jason, Westbrook?" CDR Jamison asked. That was the first time I had heard Jason's name in front of mine. The fucking irony, with me holding the chain.

"No, CDR." I was determined to finish the story but got choked up. I wiped my face as best I could in my shackles. "It was like all I could hear was my own reaction."

"Take your time, I know it's hard shipmate," CDR said offering a reassuring smile. He placed his pen down and removed his glasses.

"He jumped towards me..."

"Who jumped up, Westbrook?"

"Gary."

"What happened next?"

"I...shot him. Instead. He turned when he noticed Jay's look. He yelled out, *SHIT! JASON!* He shoved him out of harm's way and lunged towards me...I shot him. I shot him. Two more rounds. He was protecting Jason...like you know...shielding him...shielding Jason. And...I killed that man like a coward. My grandmother showed me the papers," I said taking a moment to think about the look on her face the last time I saw her.

"What did she say?" he asked.

"Well, she has a lot to say. It's Jason who won't even write me back. It's been an entire year with no trace of him and his vanilla scent. I can't fix this either. I was guilty. I plead guilty immediately. I apologized. And I...I didn't want to see Jason on the witness stand. You think he heard me doc?"

"What's that Westbrook?"

"Me?"

PTSD

I hung my head low in bold lament, irritated yet again by the sounds of the chains as I buried my head in my forearms. I sat there wondering if Jason could forgive me. The sounds of the gun replayed loudly. The sound of fighting for the spoils of war echoed. My baby girl's last breath in my arms. Each a visual calamity fighting for space in my mind to feed the damn guilt and shame I was holding onto.

BOTTOM LINE

I toiled in my sleep over everything leading up to the shooting. What was I holding on to? My dreams, if you could call them that, featured my life detail by vivid detail. It would have made more sense somehow if it were Gary pulling the trigger. This haunted me because it *didn't* make any sense. I kept dreaming the same thing. He was the one who walked in with the gun and threatened Darius and me. He saw us in bed together and snapped. But it's just a story that appears in my sleep.

I felt responsible in a lot of ways. These dreams made me question the value of everything and everyone connected to me. More importantly, how important were they and these things to me? What would be the residual value of my life if the bullets had found their way into my chest? Would I have really spent my time living for me? Hell naw! So, I put myself on notice. Was the bottom line really in my name?

Here I am in a house, which was supposed to be a symbol of stability. This was something mama *preached* to me about for *years*. A black man holding down his piece of the pie and living the American dream. I was starting to feel trapped and this didn't feel like a home. Not to mention, this wasn't my dream. None of this was my dream. It was what I was told my dream should look like. I was doing what I was told to again, appease my parents, to somehow minimize the fact that, *heeeey, I'm gay as fuck!* This house was what I was told I was supposed to get, achieve, and maintain. However, these were gains acquired from a quick decision as a means for validation. There had to be more for me in life than collecting things I had to waste money on insuring.

My neighbors had my name in their mouths. If they didn't know me before, they know my black face very well now. One heffa even brought over a store-bought apple pie and had the nerve to throw cheese cloth over it like she spent all day in the kitchen baking it just for me. She walked up one day as I pulled into my driveway craning her neck to see what all I had. Mind you this was my first time *ever* seeing her as she mentioned how clean my garage and car were. *Yup, one of those drug dealing black darkies bringing our HOA fees up for security and gang banging our property value down the crapper.* At least that's what I imagined Apple Pie Betty would be saying at her next tea and bridge party.

I apologized for the "dreadful disturbance," which is what she called it, like I had the television volume up too loud. Shame on me for feeling embarrassed on some level before she had the gall to minimize my loss to a "dreadful disturbance." I immediately turned her right on around pie and all. I made her pregnant ass limbo under the garage door before it closed while I continued gathering my things out of the car. *God*, it was *so* worth the kee-kee. White HO!

Then there was Michael, Shawn, and Preston, my close friends. We weren't hanging out as tough as we once were. This incident changed our dynamic. I know it changed me. Life was sending us into different grooves in our young adult lives, I guess. I mean, they're still my boys and they all made sure that I was good and taken care of after everything happened. It's just the crew wasn't poppin' like it used to be.

Shawn, as far as I knew was still dating Andre, Gary's best friend who'd stop by and check on me from time to time. He spent a considerable amount of time over here, reminiscing about the old days when Gary was my baby. Dre took it hard, hell. I mean, they grew up together on the Southside, so they had more than a history. He was an only child, so Gary was like his brother. Andre was a great guy and I honestly couldn't have picked a better man for Shawn, but some things he let me in on during one of our conversations, he should have kept secret.

So, whatever he and Shawn do, I hope it's with the best intentions for one another. Shawn can be very hard to read sometimes because he covers his feelings in comedy like some damn drag queen. Chicago and its party scene was gassing him up with this sudden new popularity he inherited. Being in the scene was all that mattered at the moment and the two of us became more distant this past year. That all started when I kicked them out of the crib one night though, when I was feeling shady for good reason. Perhaps, his real beef with me will surface.

Preston was managing some high-end Boutique on the Magnificent Mile by day and designing a haute couture clothing line by night. So, we were bound to see him on Project Runway or some tea. That was his goal, and we were all in support of that. I can't wait to see my boy on TV. And speaking of hidden cameras, booty was what Michael was flickin' right about...now. That much had not changed. He is still my big bro trying to be somebody's daddy, but I couldn't have asked for a greater friend. Out of anyone who has ever said they love me, I know that dude truly means it because his love is demonstrative. He's loyal and consistent. We grew a lot closer after my sexual trauma and especially after Gary's death.

They all came to the funeral and so did a bunch of the folk from Poetic Expressions. Surprisingly, my mama checked in on me and she even sent flowers to Gary's mother expressing sympathy to the family. When Mama Larreiux called and told me, I was like *whaaaaat?* To say that I was shocked would still be a gag. Out of nowhere she's on Operation Get Jason to Texas. I feel like if I move there, it's accepting defeat, like I'm returning to my parents' house. Even though I'd have my own crib, I wasn't feelin' that. At all. Not to mention, it's going to take a little more than a floral arrangement to fix us. You can't pray the gay away then expect him to stay. I need a couple of successful visits before we talk about relocation.

I sat up in the bedding and looked over at the clock on the floor and then took a quick gander at the urn. Batman tipped over towards the side of the air mattress and sat down. He had his little tongue out panting. He did some weird bow and bark, which made me chuckle and smile. Maybe I was at peace with all of this. Shoot, I still hadn't cried. I wonder if that's normal. And, I don't know when I'll have time to do that.

I got lost studying my hands deciding on which set of fingers to let his ashes slip through. How are the ashes going to feel? Will they smear on my skin like cigarette ashes? Is he watching? What is his spirit feeling? Is he still upset with me? Wow, a few more days before I do this. I traced my right hand down towards the dark scar straddling my wrist, reminded of deaths temptation. *Nope! Can't say that I'm ready to join him*, I thought.

"It's time to go on our family trip, Batman. You ready to play with Porgy and Bess, batty boy? Huh?" I said referring to Mama Larrieux's two female Pomeranians. It's funny because in the Broadway original, Porgy was a male. He barked and jumped up onto the edge of the mattress. I scooted to the edge and played with him for a few minutes. I got up so that I could walk and feed him before getting ready. "You little playa, playa! I guess you like 'em high maintenance, huh?" I laughed as Batman barked a few times. "Oh, yeah? Well, Batman, guess what! I do too." I smiled routinely grabbing and opening a small container of Vapo-Rub. I applied a thin layer around my nose.

Chicago would soon be a done deal, literally. I was making a drastic change to just...GO! I hadn't moved in years, and I had that itch now more than ever. In military speak, it was time to PCS, which means make a Permanent Change of Station. I stood staring at an urn full of Gary's ashes sitting in the window seal. My house...this house was the last place his remains resided before the family and I were to take him to the Bahamas to carry out their family tradition of releasing the ashes into the wind over the ocean. They do it a year after the death. The remains are passed from house to house for a period to allow the loved ones an opportunity to grieve privately with the spirit of that individual. It is said that it's an opportunity to reflect on good times and tough times. One last time to clear the conscience for God's continued blessings in that spirit to flow. The life is celebrated and the dust you were created from can be washed, renewed, and returned to the Earth peacefully for a future generation to be conceived.

I thought it was a very interesting practice and remembered a time Gary and I talked about what our funerals would look like after we lived to be a hundred and twenty, of course. He was adamant about being cremated. I never questioned the authority behind it, but now I understand the depth. His mother said that I had to come since I did such an excellent job speaking at the memorial service. I was urged by the family to write another poem to honor him for the occasion.

Lately, I was having trouble-putting pen to paper. I couldn't carve out time to do it and I think I was keeping myself busy on purpose. I wasn't hanging out with the crew and life wasn't as normal without my two favorite men to care for. I have written all types of poetry, but I couldn't think of anything to say to Gary in spirit at this point. Plus, I hadn't quote unquote bonded with the urn. Hell, I barely even looked at that thing. I took a minute to stare at it. It was a nice deep green ceramic-coated casing with gold accents. Gary Waddell Larrieux was inlayed in gold lettering along the top. I was amazed that all the man he was fit into a canister the size of a jewelry box.

My thoughts shifted to a memory of this one time he was sick as a dog. He was a horrible patient and would become the biggest baby when he decided to "admit" he was sick. His tantrums could be cute sometimes, though. This time, however, was far from cute. He needed to take an antibiotic and was fighting me because he didn't want the medicine. I had to fight him back into bed because he wanted to try to go to work. Then he felt like he could sweat out the sickness at the gym. He wouldn't eat, he wouldn't sleep, wouldn't take the herbal medicine Mama Larrieux brought over, he was irritating. It takes a lot to get me mad and I forgot exactly what he said or did, but whatever it was he pissed me off so bad, I yelled, *"Keep playing and the only thing you gon' get is a viewing and a burial! No dust in the wind for you buddy! At all!* I didn't realize just how bad his feelings were hurt. He literally did not speak to me for two solid days. He barely even looked at me, which was killing me, because I loved to run my mouth with him. He was not feeling me.

I kept nursing him back to health with a kiss on the cheek before I caught some sleep. I always wanted him to know I was there to help him be strong. Eventually he pulled me close to him and accepted my word to never disrespect his family's tradition like that again. Holding his ashes reminds me that he'll never hold me again. What will I have of him to visit from a visual standpoint? What about my family's tradition, Gary!? We bury our loved ones remains. There ain't even a head stone. I went through a lot with this dude in a very short amount of time it seems. Now they want me to be brave enough to not only cradle his ashes in the comfort of my hand, but also fling him into the air like sand and confess, *Gary I miss you...*

This house doesn't feel right marking quiet days of me simply coming and going. I've been moonlighting a lot lately. I'm never here. It's been a year since I slept in that bedroom. I can't get rid of the smell of his blood. I missed the way we felt in that bed. I missed waking up for work with him pulling me back into his arms for just five more minutes. I missed smelling the fire station on him when I'd greet him at the door. I missed sitting Indian style on the floor facing one another playing Jenga. I missed lying in between his legs with my headphones on scratching words into one of my notebooks. I missed being turned on by him reading the Chicago Tribune cover to cover to have something to talk to his dad about other than sports when we'd go visit. I missed tracing his body with my fingers and massaging his shoulders and lower back after he got in from the gym. I missed his post workout aroma. I missed him.

I moved all my clothes out of the space and slept downstairs in silence. Batman and me. I've been praying for peace and joy a lot lately. I'm starting to see that this trip is the right idea for something good to begin again. And that keeps me hopeful and a little scared. I'm scared in an effective way, though. I've had that feeling before and it felt good. I started selling my stuff a few months ago. What I couldn't sell, I gave away. The only thing I had left to do was to close on this house. It was a matter of paperwork and a signature. I didn't want to stay here anymore. Michael was going to come over to help me bring the last of my belongings to the storage unit this morning. The only things I had were a few books, pictures, clothes, and my Mac and all essential Apple products. I was going to sell the car, but since it was paid for due to my accident over a year ago, I opted to store it for a few months until I figured out my life.

I managed to stay strong the whole funeral and even got up to speak. It was a rehearsal of what I had written. I didn't want to appear tragic, so I kept what I said neutral because there was no pronoun to capture my personal feelings. I wasn't ready for this type of "all of a sudden." So, at the funeral I don't remember if I was a Stepford version or myself because the whole thing was a blur. I was on autopilot numb from life taking things from me. I've learned not to get use to stuff. I can't tell you how many items I have loved to death and called my favorite things only for those things to be lost moving around the globe as a kid. I never thought I'd lose people the same way I lost things. Taken. I took a deep breath and coughed as the strong smell of bleach in the air stung my nose. *People aren't things*, I thought.

I felt compelled to uproot and just leave everything and everyone I know behind. Something kept telling me I had to do this for me. What I was living was someone else's dream, not my own. *Go out and live yours!* So, I started to trust that voice. My life has been calling me. This time, loudly!

Michael thought I was losing my mind. Hell, maybe I was, but it was mine to find. He was like, *how you gon' eat, bae bro?* The answer to that question came when I received transfers into my account from two insurance companies. Gary had me listed as his beneficiary. One from his job and the other from some company his mom said he had for years with the family. I had him on my insurance, but I guess I didn't really think about something ever really happening. And even after what happened in my bedroom and with the market spiraling down, my house sold for a few more stacks than I was asking for. Things just kept coming together. So, I think it's time to forgive myself for trying to smile again.

"Come on, batty boy...!"

BIG BROTHER MICHAEL

Shits been doing Jason pretty dirty for a nice lil' chunk of time. I swear this boy is made of Teflon or just built like one of them ol' circus clown balloon thangy's, that you punch an' it come right back up. Then his plans are always extreme with this attention to detail and execution like, whoa. I thought I was anal, no pun intended, but I still get him to help me prep my uniforms for inspection 'cause he used to always get a grade of Outstanding. Jason loved that Cracker Jack uniform.

I have always admired the way he reacts to things in his own strategic prissy sorta way. If our boy Shawn is the ghetto girl of the group, then Jason is our honorary white girl. Everybody wants to be the white girl, but er'body don't want to do the work to be her. That's probably because he grew up with all kind of races.

My thing is, what black dude you know just up and quits his great paying job where he sets his own hours, supposedly sells all his shit, his house, his Beamer, to become a beach bum. When he tol' me, I was like, *Jason, you is trippin', shawty! Fuck outta here!* Now, I say supposedly, only 'cause I don't believe it. Well just yet. It's still some black in him somewhere. I'd expect my half white ass to pull some bull jive like that, but a part of me know I shouldn't doubt Jason's spontaneous, it's either black or white ass. He cracks me up! That's my lil' brother right there, though. I'm gon' hate to see him leave, but I think I've spit enough game for him to make it on his own. I always thought he was special.

I met Jason back in my Camp Lejeune, North Carolina days. We was at what was supposed to be this card party. Maaan, my first thought was, *I know I'm here to buss' sum spades, but boy looky here. A nut'll do*. I remember rubbing my hands together staring at dat ass as he walked to the kitchen. I was like yeah, that's gon' be my barrack's booty. I even cornered him one good time to let him know I was watching with that nice body of his. I laughed thinking how cute it was when he was like, *mmph, so you nasty*. I ain't know that was his slick way of calling me a ho. Him an' dat mouth.

The more I got to know him, the more I wanted to look out for him. I mean, he ain't know how attractive he was and was cautious but curious as hell. He doesn't play a tough guy cause bae bro' is a tough guy. And when he's threatened, he reacts like he doing now, on pure impulse. Kind of like how he shocked the shit outta me and Preston year befo' last when he beat this nigga ass on top of the man car. Them Midwest boys is built different from southern boys like me, they calculate then move. We just make moves and thank about the shit, later.

Jason gon' keep you guessing and this here ain't no different. Plus, I'oughnt know how he kept it together, 'cause your boy would be losing his shit right about now.

BIG BROTHER MICHAEL

And oddly enough that's one of the things I appreciate about him. It's more to Jason than most people realize, and I think he is about to figure that out for his self and I'm proud of my bae bro fo'dat. I did my part to help preserve him, so I know whatever's next, God got him.

As much as I couldn't really stand foolio he was with, my heart and condolences did go out to the family. My heart doubly so to Jason 'cause he really loved that man. I don't know if he cried at home or if he even cried at all. I cried jus' seeing how strong this boy stood at the podium sending his man off with that charming raw delivery that only Jason can get away with. He got a way with them words. And it's like his dimples are the quotation marks adding a little spice to what he be sayin'. He hasn't really said much about Darius and I haven't asked. He loved both them fools, man. Probably equally which I ain't know was possible.

I worry about him though, but I'm sure he worries about me more 'cause he's been there in some of my more critical times. Like when I found out I had to take meds for this HIV bull jive. Man, Jason made it a point to come find me and help me get myself and my place and my life back on course. He came to check me out. He didn't even harp on the issue. He just stepped in and helped me. He may come off cold as shit, and a little self-righteous, but it's a bunch of love mashed in them ice chips on his shoulders. And I will always appreciate him for that because I never told him he saved my life that day.

I caught myself thinking 'bout this time during pride, I was drunk as shit! My dumb ass got arrested for pissing in the middle of Spring Street in Atlanta to show this cutie how big my dick was even on soft. I call myself impressing him with how far I could piss. I shot my piss the length of a Jeep Commander. At least that's how the story goes. I don't remember all that. Shawn and them said he pleaded with the night watchman to give me my dose of stay in the world pills. Jason bailed me out so my mama and my command wouldn't find out, but they told him it would be another ten hours before they could release me. And we still needed to get me back to Great Lakes, so I could report for duty.

He stressed the importance of the medication and didn't leave until the cop budged on the issue. I thought the shit was a joke or they were trying to poison me at first. But when the cop walked back with Jason's phone and a legit explanation, I was cool. He handed me the pills, a tiny cup of water, told me to say cheese for Jason and walked out the cell. They went on ahead and released me like twenty minutes later. I don't know what Jason said to the po'po, but I walked away scotch free. He had us floatin' up the road in the 'Lac with me, Shawn, and Preston all knocked out. He got us back an hour before I had to report for duty.

BIG BROTHER MICHAEL

Then when I lost Momma, he was there. He wrote this real tight poem for me in this real nice Mahogany card. He was the first one to see about me and stay with me. Man, until I started actin' an ass and fought him up out the crib. I was gon' miss my best friend, man. Folks like him in your life don't jus' happen every day. Folks like him are there for a reason. We had gotten so close these past seven years, so I don't know what I'm gon' do with myself when and if he leave.

I can admit that sometimes I feel attracted to him, but I know it's a deeper type of love than me jus' wantin' to beat gut's. And I'll never take it there. Jason is one of the good ones and when you recognize that in another man, you help him preserve that, especially if he one of the good boys. I'd like to think every man like me has one on his list that he protects as his own, but never tries. That one special guy that represents a symbol of hope after we run through all the boys we run through. I'ought want to mess that shit up. I know it's a good one out there for me. I'm glad I learned that early and didn't turn him out because loyalty is hard to come by with gays. I look at it as my way of giving back to that gay marriage movement bull jive.

I was on my way to help him put some stuff "in storage" and then I was gon' take him out for lunch with Shawn and Preston. I hadn't had time to stop past his house the last couple of weeks and the last time I was there, he had shit everywhere. It looked like he was remodeling, to me at least. When he called and told me the place was empty, I had a tough time believing it. He was a day or so away from this mystery move out date he ain't said nothin' about. So, I know this boy about to tell me that he changed his mind or he went and bought new furniture because everything reminded him of Gary.

Shit yeah, Jason ain't going no place no time soon. Chicago was his big 'Love Jones' wet dream. He was Nia Long and Gary ol' blockheaded ass was Larenz Tate. Ever since he saw that movie, he was stuck on channel Chicago. I almost changed my orders 'cause I was *tied* of hearin' bout Chicago. Honestly, I didn't like it when they moved in together, but shit, I had my say and I had to respect his mind. You don't just walk away from a dream, do you? I parked the Bootillac, that's my Escalade, in the driveway. Jason had the garage open. I walked through opened the door and saw nothing but walls and floors...

"Jason, you really doing it! This boy called my fuckin' bluff," I said walking into Jason's empty house. Pine Sol and bleach filled the air, "I didn't believe you at first! But damn, these echoes make it hit home! I'm so used to coming in here asking you to turn the music down. What about the Beamer?"

"Umm, it's *Bimmer.* It's a car, not a motorcycle. It'll be in storage," he said, taping a box closed.

"Whatever car booty. How are you feeling?" I said stomping my feet listening to the sound bounce off the walls. I was trippin' off my echo.

"Mike. I'm not going to lie. I really don't know how to answer that question these days," Jason said. He was breakin' down an air mattress but stopped to look around. He had a little bit of sweat on his forehead.

"I guess that's fair," I said.

"Is it, now?" he chuckled.

"You know you don't have to leave the place spic and span, right?" I smiled taking in a deep breath teasing him. The boy's OCD was unruly. I shook my head and noticed he was barefoot. He always wears house shoes.

"I still smell his blood in here," he said without missing a beat. I didn't know what to say but...

"So why now? I mean, fuck! For real, Jason? You givin' up yo' house and just gon' up and leave the country for how long?" I asked. I needed him to really level with me on this one. I mean shit yeah, I know he just went through some traumatic issues, but this was too extreme for me.

"Like, I haven't felt this free in...well...never, Michael," he said. I realized that I ain't seen him smile in a long time. "I mean, okay it's like this. I haven't been in tune with myself. I forgot what drives me. All I remember hearing is POW, POW, POW, HE'S GONE! POW, POW! And life turns...a changing page of mind, in five-gun shots."

"Free?"

BIG BROTHER MICHAEL

"Yes, free hag! Gary and Darius are both gone. Like literally. Gone bro. I need to take that as a sign to hit the reset button...and there it is," he said looking at me before closing his eyes. He let his head fall back and sighed.

"I guess I haven't got to that point in life yet. Have you thought about every single detail like you always do? Or is this one of your impulse buys?" I said giving him the big brother shake down.

"Michael, I sold my house," he said stopping what he was doing to look me in the face. "I am just waiting for the realtor to call me to the round table with the attorneys. This is happening," he said looking around.

"Okay, so you...Jason, you know they kill faggots in the islands, right?" I said using a scare tactic. I was shook. I was expectin' this shit to be for play-play.

"Since I'm not a faggot, I don't think I have anything to worry about. Besides, this isn't a Terry McMillan novel okay? No sex on this sabbatical," Jason said winkin' at me being his normal dodgy self. He was still puttin' this shit together and retracing his steps. I know him.

"Well, tell me something, bae bro, have you cried yet?" I asked folding my arms. "To really clear your head," I smirked when he stopped and turned away from me. He ain't say nothing. He just walked over to the window and changed into a shirt he had on a hanger. I noticed how cut and lean he was as he buttoned it closed. It added to his boyish sex appeal.

BIG BROTHER MICHAEL

"You're an asshole. Out of all questions, that's what you ask, Michael?" He spoke to my refection in the glass. I stepped in closer.

"It's an important question, Jason! Because I know you! Or at least I thought I did. You jus' leaving! You giving up your possessions like you didn't work hard for all this! Nigga! You made it! And everything is changing too fucking fast. Not just your mind! This is too much! I jus' need to know that your changes are healthy. Call me selfish, but I need to know you better than good. So yeah, have you cried yet, Jason? Brothers ask questions like that!" I said not sure if saying all of that was the right thing to do. But I was worried 'bout shawty.

"Calm down. I'm going to be fine. I'm just gonna let things happen organically and..." he said before I interrupted.

"Organically?! So basically, make shit up as you go? Maaaan, you do realize you can't just bounce around through life all willy nilly with a Post Office Box for an address, right?!" I said. He turned my way.

"MICHAEL! You're correct! I don't know! I don't need to have it all planned out right now this second, this minute, in an itinerary, for you, my mama, the Navy, or these racists ass white fools I live around! None of what happened was on my schedule. I need to listen to what I want for a change! That's the change you're seeing. This old way of thinking and living isn't working for me! I came up on a lick and I'm following MY instinct! I'm out this junk! I don't have any tears to cry right now! Flat out! So, stop being so anxious to check the Jason's OK box. I'm not a damn widow," he looked at me with a serious look on his face. His hand was pressed into his chest.

"Are you okay?"

"NO! I'm not okay. Nothing makes sense these days if you can't tell. So get off my dick!"

"Goddamn! Sorry, bae bro."

"Don't be sorry. The more I think, the more I'll hesitate. I appreciate you looking out though. Okay?" He tapped my arm with the back of his hand. "Thanks for being the only top left standing in my life. Tyra will be holding your photo at the foot of the driveway before the credits roll," he said rolling his eyes as he walked away.

"You just make sure you keep that Sprint bill paid, 'cause you still talkin' out the side of your neck. Maybe this will sound better to me over the phone," I said trying not to smile. I nodded my head. He picked Batman up and gently placed him in his kennel and gave him a biscuit. I ain't know what else to say really.

"I'll be back soon, Batty boy, okay? See you later," he said shutting the cage. He stood up and walked into the kitchen to wash his hands. "You done being dramatic?"

"Now I'm dramatic?" I said.

"I don't need y'all worrying about me. I'm going to be so good," he said. I was doing all I could to feel happy for him. I just get scared when life changes. I was tearing up jus' a little bit and he shook his head and grabbed a shoebox. He sighed and said, "They do not make Tops like they used too. Ol' sensitive butt."

"Shut up! These OCD fumes in the air got my eyes waterin', that's all," I said joking with him clearing my eyes. "Talm'bout crying. Nobody cryin'. You the one need to be cryin'. I'ought care what you say..."

"Blame the bleach. Sure," he said, ignoring my statement. He sat the shoebox on top of two small boxes with the word books written on the sides. "Grab those over there. This is it."

"Damn, you won't playin'!"

"Boy, you know I'm a minimalist," he replied.

"True, true. Why else did you need to go on base?"

"I got permission to visit Darius in the brig before I leave," he said taking a breath. "For some reason, he is a special case. I wasn't really paying attention. I stopped listening with a series of *ahn huhn okay's* after the fish I was on the phone with told me I was approved," Jason said. I grabbed the boxes marked kitchen and followed him out to my truck. I popped the tailgate and we put the boxes inside. Jason grabbed the shoebox and ran back up the porch to close and lock the door. We both climbed inside.

"What you going to see him for?" I asked sucking my teeth.

"Don't start."

"What you got to say to that dirt bag?" I asked chastising him.

"He is not a dirt bag. I just need to say good-bye and get my closure before I leave," Jason said putting his seatbelt on. I turned the key to start the engine, put it in gear, and backed out the driveway.

"Right, shipmate, he's a murderer. How is the murderer doing, anyway?" I smiled and glanced over at Jason, who was not smiling back. I was kind of joking but not really.

"Ah, ah. Don't do that. And to answer your question...I don't know. I haven't seen him since I went to his hearing. He has to serve time in the brig and then Illinois State Penitentiary after his brig sentence.

"Damn, that's riiiight! That is how it works, a double whammy. Damn!" I said swerving to avoid a pothole.

"Uh huh. Man, my heart went out to him because I know him. But I don't have anything to say to him. Not yet really. I have these letters he sent week after week. There is nothing he can say to change what happened." I came to a stop at the intersection and looked over at him.

"Jason," I said wanting him to turn and look at me. I remembered how close he was to Darius and how often the two of them would write each other when he was deployed.

BIG BROTHER MICHAEL

"What up, though?!" he said turning his head to look at me. I know he was holding back his true feelings. And it sounds like he ain't trying to deal with them.

"I'm proud of you for real. This is huge and I'ma miss you man. You gettin' a chance to just go where life takes you and follow your heart for the fuck of it. I know God got you or you wouldn't be going. But I ain't gon' sit here and promise you I ain't gon' worry. I'ma try not to. But I love you, Jason. You sure you want to do this?" I said looking at and tapping the box. The car behind me laid on the horn. I looked in the mirror, rolled my window down, and flicked her off. "I know you ain't gon' miss this shit! Impatient ass bitch!" I said rippin' off through the intersection.

"Nah, I ain't going to miss that." He was staring out of the window.

"Summertime in the Chi," I said smiling blurting out a quick statement. I was debating on whether to ask my question again.

"Yeah, I know right."

"Buss'down season! Time fah' flossin' dese new skates and tossin' dem cakes, I'm try'na told'ya!" I said. He stared at me for a few seconds studying my face. I looked over at him, and then fixed my eyes to the road. I slammed on brakes at the light and noticed Jason was still looking at me. I smiled, like ain't shit happen as the truck rocked back and forth. "What, Jason, shit?!"

BIG BROTHER MICHAEL

"I'm not even going to ask you to de-country-fy that affirmation," he said finally laughing. "I'm going to assume you're referring to your new rims and sex."

"I'ma DSGB! Mind yo' own, you'll lih' long, fam!"

"You know you come back country as hell every time you go home to visit, Mr. Cox." He said.

We both laughed and kind of mellowed out for a little while. I was thinkin' bout what to say next. I think this is the first time we ever had this much none talk between us. I missed his laugh and it was good to finally see him do it. I ain't really notice until we were good and, on the freeway, that Jason had dozed off. He had the window cracked with his hands securely on the white ALDO shoebox resting in his lap. I turned the air down just a bit and reached over and let his seat back for him.

What could Darius have possibly written to Jason damn near everyday of the week judging by the size of this overstuffed shoebox? How can you console someone after you kill they damn boyfrien'? Jason a good one 'cause I prolly would'a set them shits on fire and pissed on the ashes in the middle of the Mag Mile. Shit yeah, now that would be worth a trip to jail. I should ask him to let me do that.

What could he say? Hell even that ol' fuck nigga, Gary, rest his soul, was smart enough to realize, anytime you meet a cutie who's a sweetheart, who owns his own shit, and got some tight HIV negative booty this day and age, you don't fuck that up! He ain't hafta' kill that man. I wish I could get inside Jason's head 'cause I'm missin' a few vital pieces to this madness, especially why he was so STUPID over Gary ass!

We all had our issues with Gary, especially me, because Jason lost his tough shell around him. He wasn't Jason, he was *Jason Yes Dear No Dear.* But they say that's what we all want, to be goo-goo gaga in love. On the low, I think I was rooting for Darius ol' punk ass.

Other than that, if this is what momma meant when she was explaining what it looked like to walk by faith. I think it is safe to say my best friend is doing that and I don't even think he knows. I took a good long look at him. I pray he walks into the happiness he deserves. But really easy, though. And God I hope he don't regret giving this man these letters back Jesus...

BIRDCAGE

I cleared my throat ready to speak. Someone coughed in the background just as the door swung open allowing sunlight to pour in through the rear of the church. I saw rain pouring outside through the windows, influxed with the tears being cried, to my left and my right. The creaky old church floor squealed and crunched beneath the soft footsteps of the family as they viewed the body for the last time. The steady pitter pat of rain married well with the somber sniffles of emotion saturating the sanctuary. My eyes peered towards the rear of the church and the man standing there motioned for me to come to him. Thunder and lightning instantly gave way.

I felt myself moving slowly towards the door as the sound of rolling thunder faded into the background. I turned my head, drawn to an image I saw dimly lit in one of the small windowpanes. There stood Gary surrounded by the memory of our second week together in our new crib. The furnace and the gas were out, and it was snowing fluffy toy poodles outside. We made the best of the situation because we wouldn't be able to get any assistance until the following day at only God knew what time.

Luckily, I had bought this kerosene heater at a flea market Gary's eldest sister Wanda took me to before we moved in together. He clowned me when I brought it home with the pump and kerosene, saying we'd never need that old thing. But he was grateful we had it that night. I cooked some links, peppers, and potatoes on that thing. I also made up some popcorn with some seasoned salt. Gary asked, *Where did your bourgeois ass learn hood survival techniques?*

I told him that back in the day before Daddy joined the Army, things were a little tight and we had to do what we had to do for a minute until they could get it together. My parents turned those into some awesome times and interesting learning experiences. I remember how nice it felt to just be all each other had. And how important that was. Mama was in nursing school full time. We used our kerosene heaters to heat our bath water, cook on, and stay warm together in one room. I hate taking baths to this day because of how tiring it is to play the waiting game for water heated on one of them things, especially after doing homework.

I learned to appreciate what I have for as long as I can have it. Change can happen in a moment's notice forcing you to be resourceful. Gary respected that and said he could see why I was so ahead of schedule for him. When he tasted the food, he was smacking his lips like, *Yeah, yo' ass is from Detroit. Ol' ghetto self! Let's make smores for dessert, babes!* His way of clowning me again, talking about how Detroit brothas know how to weather any storm but are stuck up. I just laughed it off like whatever.

We were with no gas for another day, and it was kind of sad when they finally came out to solve our problem. I really enjoyed that weekend...

"Hey, Jason! Wake up! We 'bout to go through the gate," Michael said shaking me up out of my sleep. I rolled my eyes at him on the verge of reading him as I adjusted the box on my lap. I pulled the visor down wiping my face to get my scene together, pausing to see if I could remember what I had just dreamed.

"Dang, I'm sorry, Michael. I didn't mean to leave you hanging. I haven't been getting much real sleep lately," I said looking over at him as he got his ID card ready and smiled. I yawned and enjoyed a good stretch. I was glad he was going up here with me to do this. It really meant a lot.

"You a'ight, you must'a been tired 'cause you was knocked out before we even hit the expressway," Michael said as I glanced over and smiled at the gate sentry. He was all Michael's type clad with smooth pretty dark skin, pretty white teeth, square jaw, and long bowed legs navigating their way up to a phat high booty. Yup! Just the way he liked them.

"Michael that was all you," I said tapping his chest. "I'm surprised you ain't say nothing to prime him." This was not normal Michael behavior and I was going to get to the bottom of that tea later. Something fishy is floating in the Kool-Aid.

"Naw, I'm good, this is about you today, bae bro," He smiled as I gave him the side eye. Now I really knew something was up. *About me, though?* I thought to myself. It was always about him.

We drove through the base and I noticed that everything looked as manicured and well put together as it did when I left active duty a few years back. This was an Admiral's base, meaning an Admiral resides in command and residence on station. Great Lakes, Illinois is home to the Recruit Training Command for the world's greatest Navy. We drove to the rear of the base towards the Brig and it didn't really hit me as to where we were going until it hit me. I couldn't believe I was going to see someone I knew in chains like an animal. I mean when you are in boot camp you hear all types of stories about the Brig and how the inmates are treated. All the scare tactics they pump into your brain about it are enough to keep you squared away. It's supposedly the military on steroids. But to me, it's almost a shame to call them inmates because the folk locked up were once our shipmates before life happened.

I'd make sure to never make them feel less than equal when the Master at Arms (MA's or Navy Military Policemen) would bring them into the clinic for treatment. I did what I could to prolong their stay and talk with them to at least try to remove their minds from their own devices. I didn't have any expectations on how I wanted this visit to go. I just wanted to face him and tell him goodbye. Maybe explain why it took a year for me to reach out. I know it may be me turning my back on him, but I hope deep down this goodbye isn't my final closing salutation to him.

The Brig was located in a secluded section of the base. It's a cylindrical building surrounded by towering steel fences topped with barbed wire. Michael parked in a spot close to the entrance and asked if I wanted him to come inside with me. I nodded my head yes and reached over to release my seat belt. I reached for my wallet and pulled it out to grab my license. I told Michael to just bring the key to his tuck and his ID as I removed my earrings. I emptied my pockets and opened the door to get out. I tucked the shoebox under my arm, and we walked up through the gate and waited to be buzzed into the visitor's corridor.

We showed our ID's and were told to walk over to a table and remove our shoes and belts and any items in our pockets. The MA looked through my box and sent it through the scanner. A police K-9 sniffed the contents and barked once. He closed the box and had us walk through the scanner. We handed our ID's to one of the guards and mine was flagged for some reason. He came over and grabbed my belongings walking Michael and I into a room near the checkpoint. He then handed us each a red visitors badge to pin to our shirts. A few minutes later, this older female officer who looked like Glenn Close stormed in to give us her elaborate motivated military introduction.

"HM2 Williams! There you are. How are you? I'm Captain Frasco, commanding officer of this fine Navy facility you're standing in! Welcome to the birdcage gentlemen," she said with great enthusiasm. She shook my hand and then Michael's and focused back on me. She handed each of us our ID's.

"It's nice to meet you, ma'am. Did I...uh, do something wrong? Pardon my confusion," I said looking at her strange and wondering why the Commanding Officer of the Brig would want to take a minute to talk to a civilian. Maybe they transferred Darius and I was too late. I slid my license into the side pocket of my jeans.

"Do you mind if I steal your friend here for a moment's notice," she said asking Michael as she gripped my shoulder. Michael nodded his head and she offered him a seat and told the guard to get him anything he wanted. Michael hated military policemen. He hated cops period. So, I knew he was going to try to work the hell out of this MA as if he were his personal assistant all because of her order. I chuckled at Michael who smiled and winked at me. And the little guy was an E-3 and light skinned. Yeah, this guy was batting a thousand today.

"Come with me doc. We're going to take a walk," she said putting her arm around me escorting me towards her office. "You were fresh out of boot camp in Okinawa, Japan, when you came onboard that Gator Freighter to assist in those oral surgeries with Lieutenant Commander (LCDR) Price. There was a blood draw I remember you helped with. And you cleaned my teeth and a few of the guys from my unit. You actually took the time to show me how to floss each one of the suckers correctly. I took your advice, HM2. I disciplined myself, and at my last few check ups the doctor told me I'm doing an outstanding job now with my oral care. No cavities this visit. No inflamed gums this visit. I only needed a polishing. I'll never forget you though. You gave me the best damn cleaning I ever had! I didn't feel a thing. You saved my teeth, shipmate! You should be proud! Good boots, outstanding uniform. Just an all-around outstanding squared away Sailor," she said as we walked into her office. She offered me a seat and walked around to her large plush burgundy chair and got comfortable. CO chairs always seemed to be burgundy. And big for no reason.

"I'm glad I could be of service, ma'am." I said not really knowing how to respond. In my mind, I was thinking, CHILE! I'm not here to exchange sea stories. But you never know who is paying attention to you and what type of impression you leave on folk. I held the box in my hands tightly. Her phone rang and she held up a finger and answered it. I thought back to those times in Japan and smiled.

BIRDCAGE

"What you got for me?... Uh huh. Okay... That's fine... You tell Simms, NO! Tell Hamilton ehhhh, again I'll consider it!... He's gotta improve that detail we spoke of some more... Tell the COD... Roger that! Tell LT Phelps his leave chit was approved three days ago. Therefore, he has two more days to finish his PQS before I reverse my decision... Put Westbrook in room 6 when you get a chance. He's on schedule. Page a code when my request has been issued, Roger...?... Alright thanks! Good job, Johnson," she said hanging up the phone. Sometimes I missed the cut and dry dialogue of the military. Boom, boom, boom, carry out the plan of the day. "Would you like a hard candy? They're sugar free," she smiled and winked.

"No, thank you. Is this customary before a visit?" I asked out of curiosity. I wasn't trying to be disrespectful, but I wanted to know why I was set aside and pulled into her office. I didn't need a white woman to pat my head like her lap dog. I needed to deliver this package and check in with this realtor. Plus, I was hungry.

"No, not at all. I rarely interfere with the visits. I encourage them to stay in contact with family and friends, especially the ones who get transferred to the state. Which is why I reviewed your background check as I do all visitors and I kept asking myself why does your name resonate with me and when I saw your picture I said well golly gee, that's the little cute squared away dental tech who cleaned my teeth haze gray and underway. I read the report on Westbrook, my heart went out to ya because I know what that's like, shipmate," she said turning a picture on her desk completely around for me to view. "That's my late partner in the picture here," she tapped the top of the frame. "And that's my little granddaughter here."

"I'm sorry to hear that, ma'am," I said offering my condolences. I looked back at her and she continued.

"Oh, thanks, but it's okay. You learn to move forward. I was stuck in the house for God knows how long. Work and home was my routine," she paused. "It got easier as I started living again for me, and not us. You just find a way to stand and then walk. Hey, I almost ran, but eventually I married my new partner. Been that way for two years. Travel and explore with my granddaughter. Put my son through college. But I just wanted to find out how you were, and just tell ya what a great man I think you are. And then to come here and face your attacker, oh boy, I just had to speak to ya," I was picking up a bit of Wisconsin in the way she talked and by her personality. She was charming if not intuitive. "What brings you in to see Westbrook today?"

"I'm simply here to return his letters personally. I don't want to read about how sorry he is because it won't change anything that has already happened, so this is goodbye," I said not wanting to go into too much detail.

"I see. I understand you were at his hearing..."

"Yes, as a proxy for...Gary. Just to see justice served for him," I interrupted.

"So, you are aware of his fate?" she asked looking at me with concern spiraled down her face.

"Yes, Captain. I was there and I understand his sentence," I answered as a page to her office interrupted my flow. She pushed the button on her phone and a voice announced: "Code stillroom six, ready out." I let out an audible exhale expressing my irritation.

"Roger," she said releasing the button. "Let me be frank, HM2. I don't know him like you do. But I know people. I have a background in criminal law as well as psychology. After his evaluation...I just want ya to know he is not the same man. You know him as Darius, but he is not the same Darius you knew before things took a turn for the worst. Not right now at least. Are ya really ready to see him?"

"I'm ready to se..." I started before she interrupted me.

"Because if you are his friend, then you won't judge him. You'll continue to be as much of a friend as you can be right now for him, okay? And pray for your shipmate. He's still our shipmate. If nothing else let him still be that to ya HM2, okay? Because this PTSD thing with him goes much deeper than the war. There may be some answers to a lot of your questions in those letters. I promote healing and I *encourage* letter writing here at this facility. It relieves some of the pressure. That's all I'm at liberty to say," she said warning and preparing me at the same time. I started to have second thoughts. Would I regret this decision?

"I can do that," I said closing my eyes and offering a polite smile. I kept trying to convince myself this needed to happen. I started practicing what I was going to do and say in my head about that time.

"Okay, let's head down. Let me give you a hug. You're a brave man, HM2. I'm proud of you for staying strong," she hugged me, patted, and rubbed my back. "Here's my card. Stay in touch if you'd like. Off the record I'll keep you abreast on certain particulars," she said releasing me. She smiled, nodded, and placed the card in my hand before wrapping me up in another hug. "Have a safe trip," she whispered and rubbed my back. I didn't remember telling her I was going anywhere, so I took that as a good sign.

I let go of her and she winked at me placing her arm around my shoulders. She guided me down the corridor to the entrance of the main housing unit. I slowed down when we passed the room where Michael was seated. There he was with a foot-long sub, feet propped up, and a TV I don't remember being there before. He shrugged his shoulders looking up with mustard smeared on his face mouthing the question, *What happened?* I chuckled shaking my head at him as he stuffed his face with a big smile. I walked into the room, pushed his feet off the table and sat the box next to him. "Punk ass!" he yelled, smiling looking at the box as I ran to catch up with the Captain.

She showed her ID and I reached into my pocket and did the same. The guard unlocked the door and we walked through. He rendered a hand salute and shut the door. There was a solid click and then the second door opened. We walked through that door and it immediately slammed closed with two solid clicks. The hairs on the back of my neck stood on end as if something or someone was right up on me. A cold musty gym smell became apparent. The guard rendered a hand salute and escorted us into the stillroom section of the visitor's center. He unlocked a door and the CO told me she was honored to meet me and explained the guard would escort me to the safe zone once I finished conducting business.

The guard nodded and opened the door allowing me to walk in. Darius was mumbling or singing something with his head held down. My heart started to beat rapidly as I tried not to look at him like an exhibit in the zoo. He was completely shaven. The orange jump suit made his already dark skin appear darker. He was tapping his feet and stopped once the guard closed the door. He didn't react and I didn't move. I tried to swallow and control the pace of my heart. He lifted his hands and placed them on the round metal table cemented into the floor.

BIRDCAGE

The chains they had him strapped in made him seem barbaric. My heart softened and I walked over to him, put a smile on my face, and sat down as if this was normal.

"You smell good, Jason," he complimented looking up at me. I noticed he had shaved both eyebrows off as well. He had no hair on his face or his head. I was stunned. His once smooth dark skin was ashen. It looked like he had given up on himself.

"Thank you. Darius, how are you doing?" I said hanging on to my smile. I was thinking, *What the entire hell?* He smiled back bopping his head to a melody he started humming.

"Did you bring me some moisturizer? I need moisturizer bad," he said still smiling at me.

"I'm sorry, but I didn't," I said starting to feel bad for him. His lips were dry and cracked as well. He didn't look the same. He was losing his muscle mass also. This was not Darius.

"You remember when we was on the beach that night and we was close and got quiet when that Isley Brothers' song was playing on the radio? The aroma you keep on your skin. The breeze was mixed with you. That's how you smell right now. I...ha ha, yeah buddy. And yoooo! I was scared to admit to you that I liked you. Or...no...what did your German ass say, ol' German face ass...ha ha, you remember the face ass game, Jay?" He started singing the song and beat boxing looking at me.

"Yes. I remember, Darius." I stated.

"Yeah, you remember that shit." He stopped singing and his face turned stoic. He glared at me. "Like the night you told Larry you loved him. I should have said something, man. But I couldn't...you ain't waitin' on no nigga, you ol' ain't sweatin' nigga's face ass." He got really serious, suddenly. "You get my letters?"

"Yes."

"So, where mine's?"

"Darius, I couldn't bring myself to read any of them," I looked into his eyes and saw them instantly well up with tears. "...Yet." I closed my eyes and took a breath. I didn't know what I could say next. I had pushed the door open, soooo, GO!

"Damn! You didn't read my letters I wrote to you, Jason?" he asked as the chains struck the metal table.

"I'm sorry, Darius, but what could you possibly say to me in any of those letters to change what took place?" I asked trying to stay calm. I took a breath.

"If you'd read my letters, you'd know! Damn! For real, Jason?" he said shaking his head.

"I can't do that right now," I retorted.

"This some dog ass shit, man." He looked away before continuing. "I...can't forgive myself, and you come in here smelling like you love me," he said pausing and looking around the room. His breathing became erratic and then he glared at me again. "So, you don't know that...you didn't read about my uncle? Why didn't you read them? Better yet, what did you do with them?"

"Listen, Darius! I'm not ready to relive that again. A written apology isn't going to bring him back, okay? And it isn't going to get you out of here. Don't send me any more letters, okay?" I said, still building up the nerve to tell him I was leaving with no return flight.

"Why not, Jason?! You used to like to talk to me and send me letters. Can't you wait?"

"Darius, what the *HELL* am I waiting on?! Exactly?!" I asked trying to make sense of this conversation.

"Me! You gotta wait on me!" Darius asked almost begging but smiling.

"We just pen pals!"

"I'm not a goddamn pen pal to you though?!"

"I'm leaving the country, Dee! I'm not coming back to Chicago. I am only here to tell you in person, a'ight." I said shushing him before he interrupted my flow. "Soooo! I'm going to carry out Gary's last will and testament and figure the rest out later. My dream has...died, dude," I said. He looked at me with a strange look.

"You gotta fly free like a blackbird." He hung his head and started speaking to his feet. "I'm a mission accomplished. A new patient to patch up and forget. Jason and MiMi were all I had, and he gon' drop out the race too, huh? Dad sure as hell did; he must have thought his dirty little secret was going to come out. All my little blackbirds flying out of my sight. I told the birds to fly away and that they couldn't have the torso. We had to send it home. Jason. I sent the torso home away from...away...from the blackbirds." He took a deep breath and looked up at me with more tears in his eyes. "No response...meant you really didn't read my shit. Jason, you can't *leave* me this way man! Help me get better yo'! I need you here...Jason, to not let go. I need you to talk...talk to the doctor man, you can tell him it was self-defense and, and, and, and, that because I'm a...uh uh PT and D...I got PTSD and, and, and...no, Jason, wait! I need you to stay man!"

"Me *waiting* on you Darius...and mailing you shit got him killed," I stated swallowing hard with a dry mouth.

"Fuck you!"

"Really?! Coward! *FUCK ME?!* You did! How 'bout that?!" I retaliated.

"Fuck you if you leave me here like this, Jason! Fuck you if you leave Chicago airspace, nigga. I know I fucked up. BAD! And, and, and, I know. You know what!? You was my HEART! Meeting you, Jason. DAMMIT! Changed me. You preserved the core of me. That's what I wrote!" he screamed with hoarseness in his voice as the MA opened the door and instructed me to exit the room to deescalate the situation. He walked in to try to calm Darius down. Two other guards ran over to isolate me and assist if needed. Darius stood up and then sat back down.

BIRDCAGE

He was staring at me through the window. I recall a need to touch the part of the glass highlighting his face. He looked away from me then down at the table. I was escorted back through the facility to the safe zone numb and detached from what had just happened. The Captain was right; he wasn't the same man I knew, but I knew that the night he killed Gary. A ghost of Darius came back home from the war. I just needed some time. A lot of space and time to admit some things to myself...

BEREAVED

I just knew seeing Jason would have been all I needed to fix what's going on in my head. Here I am in the dark bouncing a red rubber ball against this cold ass concrete wall. The wall is painted Navy haze gray of course. It's smaller than my old cell which housed me and another hard leg. It's cold in here at night. I usually pull my wool blanket around me to stay warm even though it makes my skin itch and feel like its crawling. That's why we call them woolly bullies. They keep you warm as fuck though.

My cellmate got transferred last week and since I'm under psyche evaluation they decided to keep me to my own cell. Being in this cell by myself gives me nothing but time to think. But man, I swear I'm about to go crazy. And that's what got me in here. They got me taking these fruit colored pills saying they'll calm me down. They feel like tranquilizers though. They hit you like a fucking train. Like, I'm in my own thoughts and then boom! I'm zoned the fuck out staring at the nothingness of my life. How can I get my mind right in a tranquilized state? Riddle me that. This shit can't calm me down. I lost everything including my mind. I'ma find that mug though. Swear to God. I'm a monster. Where my mind go yo'? How a pill gon' get my mind back?

I'm just going to keep bouncing my ball till it come back to me. Till it come back to me. Till it come back to me. It's a mind game, yup they playing with my mind, like how...the CDR was kind enough to give me something to play with other than my dick. Yeah. It's a mind thing. Okay, like how I can't get hard anyway. Damn pills! Okay, I gotta stop tripping so I can get an early out and then I can see...Jason. It must be something in the water, cause my dick ain't been hard for a minute now. Jason smelled good as fuck and I ain't brick.

I can't focus on him. I gotta focus on my ball to clear my mind. Doc cleared it with the CO. It's helping me channel my thoughts by forcing my mind to organize them in a neat flow. At least that's what the Commander says. Plus, it's Jason's favorite color. It was the first ball I saw out of all the blue and neon green ones he had in the container. It's about the size of a silver dollar and looks to be pretty durable. It doesn't make a lot of noise. Doc said it's important to start thinking about what mattered to me before I got in here so that I can have what he calls my first breakthrough. I just go in there and keep my eyelids open and try not to think about or mention or have him question...Jason.

Jason came by and pissed me off. He ain't take time to learn my story. He didn't read my apology. He should have just left, man. He made me feel disposable. Maybe I just took too much from him. Yo! I did kill his man.

I stopped bouncing the ball when I heard a baton hit the floor down the hall. I looked at my cell door and drifted off into a daydream and saw the judge at my court martial banging the gavel calling the court to attention so that he could deliver my sentence. I held onto the ball tightly like I held my fists that day. Tight like a roll of case quarters. My uniform was sharp, set off by square shoulders, with me standing at the position of attention. I concentrated on not locking my knees so I wouldn't pass out. I was thinking, keep standing, and don't fall. Face your fate. You did this.

I felt so small and I couldn't talk my way out of this situation. The word murder echoed. I was defenseless to stop it. It hit me when the arresting officer radioed *murder* over the airways after he put me in the back of the car. I remember they pulled me past Jason who was sitting in the front seat of a squad car. I tried to get his attention by apologizing as loudly as I could. He just looked at me. Jason didn't shed a tear. He just sat there. His eyes followed me all the way to the cop car. I felt so fucked up.

He looked so helpless but determined to bring that man back to life. I blacked out and was in another place. It was almost as if I was in the sandbox on watch. I reacted to movement. I pulled the trigger three times like I was on the range training with 2nd Marine Division. That's what it felt like - like he was a dark target behind enemy lines lurching at me. I saw some makeshift threat that I needed to eliminate for Jason's survival. A dude more than a shipmate. Maybe I was the threat. He was just protecting Jason and covering him from my perception.

I got opportunities to look over at Jason and MiMi during a brief recess in the courtroom. MiMi had tears in her eyes. Jason wouldn't make eye contact with me. He was either looking down or out of the window. The judge ordered me to face forward and called me back to attention. I stood there as he read each charge to include premeditated murder, murder in the 1st degree, conduct unbecoming of a uniformed commissioned officer, unlawful entry, use by deadly force, two counts of absence without leave strike 16 days, and use of an illegal narcotic substance. After my evaluation is complete at the birdcage, I am to serve the remainder of my former military contract here; then I'm to be handed off to the state of Illinois to be sentenced for murder and a few similar charges after the military is done with me.

They diagnosed me with PTSD, and I guess I can believe that. I saw some messed up shit over there in Kuwait and Afghanistan that I don't really like to talk about. I did put some of the things I went through in my letters to Jason. And now I *really* don't belong to me. I gotta do what these assholes tell me when they tell me day in and day out. The only freedom I have is a ball to bounce. The sound of the ball made my mind drift to a time when I just knew Jason and I would stay cool...

BEREAVED

One morning I woke him up way before the crack of dawn to invite him to run with me and watch the sunrise. Camp Lejeune had some of the best sunrises. So, I wanted to share a cool part of me with him to show him in my own way I thought he was special. It was the quickest I'd ever seen him get ready for anything. He had never run on sand before, so I took it easy on him. He toughed it out and I think that's when I really took notice of him. I saw him put his heart into it. The sky was the prettiest shade of orange I'd seen. I made sure to take a picture of us. Which was the one MiMi discovered. I made it my screen saver in every phone I've ever owned. It shows me standing behind him with my arm across his body all tight with a sunrise and sand framing us. I liked how he looked and felt sweating in the sun against my sweaty body.

Damn. The beach was ours that morning. The wind was blowing and shit, and we played in the water a little. That was the longest I've ever talked to any nigga about anything not being sports related or about some pussy. He got a little dirty with me and lay in the sand, and that's when I taught him the Face Ass game. I massaged his calf's and feet so he wouldn't be sore from the run. Jason put my mind at rest. I was the one who shouldn't have waited. I wonder where he on his way too. I wonder if I were free would he let me go with him? *Shit, my days aren't my days anymore,* I thought as the lights came on and Reveille was called over the intercom.

BEREAVED

I got up like a trained puppet and tightened up my rack placing my red rubber ball in a pouch I created in my pillow. I grabbed my shower kit and slid my shower shoes on my feet happy that my section was still first on the shower and sink rotation this week. They stagger each grid into the head and each section gets a week to go first. I stood by my cell door waiting for the doors to unlock so that I could rush to the head and grab a stall. The sooner you showered, the hotter the water. And I like piping hot showers especially around these filthy cocksuckers. Nasty ass mu'fucka's.

I heard the pop then the click as all doors on my row opened. I rushed out into the corridor standing at attention readying my voice to sound off. The starboard side began as my ears locked in on each man reciting his assigned cell number. I heard 24 and yelled out 25. After roll call, we state the Pledge of Allegiance in unison and render a hand salute as the National Anthem plays. Then the command to move out is given and we are able to right face and shuffle our way into the head to shit, shower, and shave. Fifteen minutes for fifty hard legs to pump and dump.

I'd always get my soap and rag ready and sit my hygiene bag on the bench closest to my favorite stall. I took my soap in hand and wet my rag before pulling the curtain closed. I always close my eyes and pretend to be in my shower at home. At home, the latest jam would be jumpin' in the background and I'd be getting ready for a bust down to come through. Sometimes I'd roll out and pick them up.

I turned the water off and grabbed my towel to dry off. The steam rising off of my dark skin felt nice in contrast to the cold AC air blasting throughout the building. I grabbed my hygiene bag and pulled my draws out of it. I slipped them on and put my jump suit back on. I sat on the bench and dried my feet and put socks on. I put my regular sneaks on, grabbed my shower shoes and bag, and walked over to a sink quietly. I pulled my toothbrush out and put some paste on it. Right when I was about to brush my teeth this crazy ass white boy walks over to the sink right next to me out of every empty sink available and says, *What's up Whoopie!?* I started to beat his ass until he bucked his eyes at me, and I noticed he shaved his off too. He told me he had PTSD as well and for some reason that was the first thing he did. Like me, he said it just felt like something was crawling on his face that he could not get rid of. He said he did it so long that when he stopped, they never grew back. He told me to stop while I was ahead. He said some shit like, *"Now, I look like that gnarly motherfucker Freddie Kruger when I get mad bro!"* I chuckled for a second.

I took his little warning to heart. His name was Chad. He used to be a SEAL onboard the USS Nimitz, one of the oldest nuclear-powered Aircraft Carriers in the fleet. After the ship got back from its Western Pacific (WestPac) cruise he came home from a nine-month deployment to a wife with two and a half months' worth of baby growing inside her. Let's just say, she'll never get pregnant again. He says it was the only recon mission he soon forgot about. I wasn't really trying to connect with anyone in here because I didn't feel like I belonged. I felt like if I could stay connected to the outside world that I would stay focused on getting out. But the reality was I was no better or no less than anyone that I was locked up with. Life has to go on for me as well and I need an outlet. MiMi said, I've never met a stranger, with my charming ass. I let Chad do all the talking at first. I wasn't ready to talk about me. I just gave him my name and nodded and agreed with his continuous banter. He was entertaining enough to say the least.

Everything in here was routine, and Chad finally broke up that monotony for me. He talked all through breakfast, which was better than listening to the alarms, buzzers, whistles, and clicks of the doors. Besides being locked up for some type of criminal activity, we were still shipmates. He came in a few weeks before me and would be transferred any day now, since his mental health evaluation was complete. I noticed how good-looking he was. He was a shorthaired blond guy with dark blue eyes. He had these cherry red lips with a little shape to them, a tight solid body and some thick ass thighs and calf muscles. I guess he had what they call the All-American look. His physique reminded me that I was slacking on my weight training. So, I may have just found a lift partner, seeing as we were around the same height and build.

I walked the corridor to the library to find a good book to read like doc suggested, but I couldn't focus on a book as hurt as I was. How could he leave me in this hell hole? To just say fuck me! Fuck Darius! Fuck my life right now! I stopped in the middle of the corridor and tucked my head between my legs. I had to get control of myself. I need...yeah, I gotta get to sick call. I need my.... yeah, if I go to sick call, I can get my meds, and that will buy me more time to interact like a normal person. I...need to relax though. The alarm sounded alerting us to get back to the racks. This pissed me off because I have to listen and respond to a damn alarm like one of them dogs in a Pavlov experiment. Only I'm not salivating and ain't no treats. *I gotta...I have to relax.* I kept my head tucked between my legs and tried to catch my breath. I leaned up against the wall attempting to get myself together.

I needed to work out again, that would be a way for me to channel my energy too...yeah! Me and that white boy can work out together, but I need to go to sick call and then I can work out. *I need to relax because I gotta get better and get out of here. And I can find out where Jason is and stop him before he moves out of Chicago. I gotta be good because they will let me go home on good* behavior, I think. I need to think. I need to think, man. THINK! THINK! Before they come over here, I thought to myself. If I stand up and keep walking...I don't want to stand. I don't have nobody to lean on right now. I was trying to will myself to stand up but my mind was someplace else. Wait I...I...got Chad! Yeah...I...Chad found me for a reason. I gotta go to sick call. But if I go to sick call, they gon' give me that...them...those nasty ass pills. I can't go to sick call. NO! I can't! NO! The pills hurt my stomach. BUT I CAN'T STOP THINKING! HELP! SOMEBODY! I got...I gotta chill. Dee, you need to stand up. And, I need my dad's pull. Yeah, I can write my dad to get me up out of here. I got to write him a...NO! He not coming.

Jason can't stay cause of what I did. But I gotta write him a letter. I can fix this, if he'll read what I have to say. But he didn't read my story, he don't know what happened. He don't know why Dad asked about him. CDR Jamison...can find him. WHERE?!

"Fuck you, Jason! Fuck you, Jason! I hate you for this shit man! I hate my dad for this. I hate...y'all for this shit," I slid down the wall and sat on the floor as two MA's responded to my outburst. My heart was pounding through my chest. They helped me up with my cooperation and took me back to my quarters. Reality hit. I stood at parade rest manning up against the pressure mounted behind my eyes. Morning routine was over and the count off began. *I'm a prisoner. This is for real.* On queue I heard 24 and immediately sounded off the number 25. I did a crisp about face and entered my cell falling to my knees. The thick cell doors rushed on their rails slamming shut in unison with the same sturdy click I used to hear on the roller coasters at Six Flags, only this ride wasn't going anywhere anytime soon. Fuck my life...

CAY

Flying into the island was a little choppy as the pilot flew around a massive storm miles from the shore. It felt like we were on a carnival ride or some junk. My first thought was something I didn't think about before making this trip. Hurricanes. I had been in a couple of Typhoon's when I was stationed with the Marines in Okinawa, Japan, so if it was anything like that, then I guess I'd be fine out here. This could be my naivety talking.

Michael's voice filled my head, *I hope they have real houses and not huts,* as if he were sitting right next to me. I remembered how ridiculous I thought he sounded and laughed silently, now thinking about Gary. I wish he were alive so I could share that joke with him. He and Mike had a love hate relationship with one another. Mike didn't think he was good enough for me, not to mention he's territorial around other light skinned brothas. Gary felt like Mike was in my head to much. His conclusion was Michael was simply waiting for his chance to fuck. My mind shifted to Batman. I hoped he was okay down in the cargo hull. I was definitely going to have to make it up to the little guy once I got settled.

I looked out of the porthole window and leaned my head against the glass breathing a sigh of relief as we circled just a few of the beautiful islands. The water was made up of these brilliant shades of blue turquoise encrusted with white-capped waves that looked like cake icing from up here in the sky. I couldn't help but stare at them wondering which day I'd be brave enough to step foot into the Atlantic again. The last time I did was when Mama took me and baby sis to Panama City beach before we left for Germany. The water was so warm. I smiled as the sun burst its way into view shining down on my new home for a while.

I pulled out my notebook jotting a few notes down, taking quick pauses to enjoy the descent onto the island of New Providence. My head bobbed to the beat from the music flowing through my ear buds even though the turbulence was trying to throw off my rhythm. I finally flipped my notebook closed when I realized what I was here to do. *God, I'm not ready to let him go. Please don't make me do this.* I thought I'd be able to write his poem on the plane, but I still couldn't think of anything. I sat back and rubbed my hands together. I closed my eyes and thought back to the stories Gary would tell me of him, his cousin Hannah, and his granddaddy.

He made the island sound so mysterious, and we'd talk about going on occasion. But with everything surrounding us, when would we make time. The last time we talked about going, he brought it up out of the blue. I was studying and he was like, *I'm working on something, babes. I'm going to love seeing your face light up with what I am going to show you.* I smiled remembering the look on his face. *Well, thank you, Gary, now what are you God getting me into?* I thought to myself.

I think we circled the islands a couple of times before we landed at Lynden Pindling International Airport. One of those small trucks with the ladder on it came and attached to the small commuter jet I flew in on. I was all smiles as I unhooked my seatbelt and swung my carry-on bag over my shoulder. I looked in my bag for my passport and my phone before getting up from my seat. The moment I stood up I got a call from Mama Larrieux. I made my way forward gliding by the flight attendant smiling with a welcoming safe stay greeting.

"Good afternoon, Mama Larrieux! How are you?" I said stepping down carefully. I looked around to see if they were unloading the bags. I was worried about Batman. I reached into my bag and put on the pair of black Ray Ban's I bought at the airport in Chicago. Michael and I used to call them *asshole glasses*. It seemed like these were the shades that all the *assholes* in the Navy wore in port. He had me cracking up with the validity of that statement. The white assholes wore them tacky Oakleys and the black assholes would wear Ray Bans. I probably looked like a tourist more so than anything with my small-framed self. Go figure.

"How are you, sweet pea? You landed safely I see?" She asked. I could hear her excitement about my arrival coming through the phone.

CAY

"Yes, ma'am, your son and I made it. I know Batman is upset with me though," I chuckled. I looked behind me one more time to see if I could see his cage being unloaded. I hope they didn't forget my batty boy.

"Yes. Lordy Lord, dey don't like them old loud planes. Poor thing was probably frightened the whole time, now! Listen, sweet pea me and Timmy is out at the baggage claim. We are waiting for ya. This Waddie callin'," she said as I let her click over. Mrs. Larrieux was back in her element. She was relaxing her dialect and letting her accent flow free. I loved listening to her speak. Her level of far out there thinking was right up there with mine. We're both Aquarians. I was sure she and I would have many more of our talks while I was here with the family.

"Okay, see you in a bit," I said walking through the terminal.

I was glad I put on some shorts instead of the jeans I was debating on wearing. This weather made you want to wear the bare minimum from just the little bit I experienced walking in off of the tarmac. Customs wasn't as busy as I thought it would be and I assume the reason is because most of the folk who visit are tourists onboard any given cruise liner in the harbor. I walked down the long breezeway with blue carpet and artwork that put you in the mind frame of sunny beaches, warm weather, and plenty of recreational activities to do on the water.

CAY

The smiles from Mama Larrieux and Gary's youngest brother Timothy relieved some of my anxiety as I put my shades into my shirt pocket. Mrs. Larrieux was sitting in a seat on the phone. Batman was sitting in her lap and he jumped up with excitement and ran to my leg as she cackled. I scooped him up and rubbed his back while he licked my cheek squirming to get closer to me.

"Awww, I missed you too, batty boy. You okay, booski?! Huh? You okay?" I asked him as he whimpered and wiggled in my right arm, still licking me as I walked up to the two of them giving each of them a hug. I sat the carry-on bag down in a chair. "How are you two doing? Man, it's so good to see you, Mama Larrieux.

"Hey, you beautiful boy! How ya feelin'?" she asked.

"I'm doing better." I said, removing the pressure jacket off of Batman to put on his harness.

"Bless Batman's little heart. Him missed Jason," she said as she pet him. I missed him too. "Here let me take him while you go find your bag," she said taking him from under my arm.

"I'll be right back, batty boy, okay?" I said smiling rubbing his snout.

"Jason, you should consider a new nick name for him while you're here," Timmy laughed. I thought about what he said and realized batty boy was a derogatory term to mean *faggot* in Caribbean culture.

"Oh yeah, maybe you're right!" I laughed as I made my way over to the carousel to retrieve my bag. Timmy walked over with me and grabbed my suitcase. He looked like a younger Gary and was just as tall. He had a similar build to his late older brother and the resemblance was very present in his smile. He and Gary were extremely close, and he took it the hardest at the funeral. He seemed to be fine now though. But looking at him reminded me yet again the main reason I was here. Watching him with my bag reminded me of Gary's visit to Raleigh when we first began taking one another seriously. We walked over to Mrs. Larrieux and I grabbed the kennel. She was holding Batman who was right at home being spoiled by her gentle touch. I rubbed his nose and he licked my finger in between pants. He had finally stopped shaking.

"Oh, look at you with the peach fuzz on that baby face of yours. You decided to grow a beard, ay?" She asked rubbing my face with her fingertips. She started smiling at me.

"Not intentionally. It's been a couple of weeks since I've shaved," I smiled. This was the first time since separating from the Navy that I hadn't shaved. It was itching like crazy.

"Jason, I am so glad you came. I just want to thank you for this. It's really sweet of you, ya know?" she said placing her free arm around me to give me a good squeeze.

CAY

"No place would I rather be right now," I said smiling at her. When we made our way to the parking deck, the tropical weather greeted us all with a kiss from the sun's rays. Birds tweeting and doing summersaults in the air were a direct contrast to the tranquil feel the beautiful scenery in the background provided.

We loaded up the car and made our way out of the airport onto JFK Road headed to Nassau so that Mama Larrieux could get the boys some straw hats for the fishing trip her husband and some of the other men were going on. She also had to get some wicks for the kerosene lamps when they go night crabbing on Exuma. The island was pretty squat with none of the buildings reaching past the Palm trees. It was as if the atmosphere was saying, *eh, why stretch when you can lie here on the beach in the sun.*

When we arrived in downtown Nassau, Mama Larrieux told me that one day while I'm here to get a feel of the history of the Bahamas and learn about the islands British Colonial background. I thought I saw black folk in Atlanta, but ATL ain't got nothing on The Bahamas. I have never seen so many types of black folk in all types of capacities in my life. Mama Larrieux gave me a brief rundown of the demographic being almost over eighty-three percent black and a quarter of them born with the blood of freed slaves seized and set free during early New World maritime trade on the Grand Island. She talked about how the pink Parliament buildings made pink her favorite color, which is why she and her oldest daughter Wanda pledged AKA.

I looked down the horizon and over to my right and got a glimpse of the ocean. I rolled my window down and rubbed Batman as he stuck his head out of the window. I started to formulate what I wanted to say to Gary in my poem. It was starting to become clearer that he was gone. A chill ran up my spine as I thought back to the night he died. Just after he was shot, he gripped me sooooo tight. My thoughts were interrupted as Timmy slammed on brakes to avoid hitting this car that moved to far out into the intersection. He blew the horn fussing and gesturing at the man.

"Calm down, Timmy, no one is hurt, and the car isn't damaged, and Jason is here safe," she said rubbing his head. I had forgotten that he is a hot head just like his big brother was. I smiled to myself shaking my head. I used to always casually calm him down after one of his road rage fits. I learned the hard way with him in Chicago traffic after he put the truck on two wheels to prove a point that arguing with him while he was mad was not going to help solve the problem.

"Yes, mom. But I just hate stupid stuff like that; they should pay attention," Timothy said smiling and shaking his head.

"I like this song, Timmy," she said turning up the volume and rocking her body. Timothy smiled as she kissed his cheek. This seemed to ease his tension.

"Mama Larrieux, what you know about this? This is before your time?" I said rubbing her shoulder smiling ear to ear. She rubbed my hand.

"Jason, that ain't nuthin' but a little Calypso set to one of them fast uptempo dance songs. You all are just discovering what's been here long before you come, young man," she said looking back to wink and smile at me.

"Alright touché." I laughed. "Timmy, I know your butt don't know nothing about this?" I teased.

"Big bro turned me on to this Electronic Music. Some of it is pretty solid," he said stopping at a red light. He turned around to pet Batman who started licking his hand.

"Yeah, that's because I turned his butt on to it," I smiled thinking how good it was to reconnect with the *in-laws*.

Batman was a happy puppy now that he was away from the scary plane. He was running from side to side poking his head through each passenger window, tongue hanging all out. I let him have his fun until the car started moving, then I made him stay on my side, so I could hold on to him. After we completed her tasks, we took a ferry over to the house. Mama Larrieux reached for Batman who surprisingly jumped in her lap. He was starting to become a little less timid and snippy around other people. I took this opportunity to enjoy the sunshine and breeze as I began scribbling the skeleton of Gary's poem. I began to think about him as the rocking motion of the ocean caused the ferry to list delicately above the churning current. The sounds of sea gulls flying overhead avoiding the smokestacks were repelled away by the blast of the foghorn. I rested my head slipping into a daydream of the last night I spent with Gary alive.

We were on our way to the rough side of town, which is the Westside of town - Albany and Kedzie in Garfield Park to be exact. Gary always teased me about being from Detroit. Talking about there ain't no danger on the Westside like there is on any side of Detroit...

"Babes, I don't know why you scared of a little Westside action. Ain't shit popping right now, but your chattering gums, I got you," Gary said as he opened the door to this famous soul food restaurant. The place at the time was known as Edna's. It's now under new ownership and has been renamed Rudy's. Thankfully, they are still preserving the sweet taste of Chicago's spin on great soul food. I turned back and rolled my eyes at Gary and smiled as I walked inside.

"Shut up, Gary! Ain't nobody scared," I said putting my hands in my pockets.

CAY

"Me keep tellin' ya, me a rude boy in love wit'a tendah foot Yankee mon!" he said making me laugh. "Look at yo' ass tensin' up and shit," he started shaking his head laughing at me again.

"What the hell ever, negro!" I said laughing at him teasing me.

"It's okay. It's been a minute since you've had to renew your street credit in the D," he stopped laughing and cleared his throat putting on a straight face and his fist up to his mouth. "If we wasn't out west, babes, I'd kiss yo' lil' sexy ass," he said in a low tone with a wink.

"I ain't sacred," I said moving in closer to him just as the waitress walked up with a great big smile. She grabbed two menus and walked us to our seats.

"So welcome to Edna's, babes!" he said with this huge cherry Kool-Aid grin smeared all over his handsome face.

"I see, so what's the hype? I mean, what's up?" I said looking around observing the Grandma Style décor and the pictures hung on the walls of the various famous politician's and celebrities who have raised a fork in this joint.

"Awhhh, babes, didn't you read the sign? We here for the best biscuits on Earth, nigga what?" We both laughed. "Well, it don't say *nigga what*, but I know you love you a good biscuit, and you know I love fuckin' up, *your* biscuits," he said giving me an extra cheesy grin.

"Yeah, nasty," I chuckled, shaking my head.

"That's what you like, though. I just thought I'd share some ghetto make-up date night biscuits with my babes!" I started cracking up as the waitress came back and sat two glasses of ice water and a basket of biscuits on the table. "Right on queue."

"Thank you," I smiled at the waiter.

"Oh, ya'll just having a good ol' time over here at this table, huh?" Our waitress Donna stated with a bright smile. "Ah, ah! What's so funny? Y'all talkin' bout my weave, or suh'in, whassup?" I laughed and covered my mouth as she smiled and folded her arms. She looked at me then at Gary.

"Yeah, my man's here was talking about how obviously fake your hair looks." Gary shook his head and looked at me and winked. He sat back in the booth gazing at me and bit his lip with this cocky smirk. I smiled at Donna, who had her hand on her hip and a stank look on her face.

"We were not discussing anything remotely close to your choice in bundles," I said crossing my heart and offering a sweet smile. She giggled and looked over at Gary.

"Umm hmm, I know! Uncle Gary plays too much," she said as he burst out laughing. I reached up and quickly tossed my spoon at him.

"My bad, I had to get you," he said, still laughing. Donna hit him lovingly.

CAY

"How you doin' though? I miss youuuu! You gotta come see the baby too! He gettin' so big for real, Uncle!" she said as she looked over her shoulder and waved at one of the male waiters.

"I will, you know that. But are *you* all right?" Gary asked with a serious look on his face.

"I'm straight, but thank you so much, Uncle Gary, I mean that. Who is this fine man sitting all across from you smiling and laughing with you and stuff? You is so ruuude uncle, ah ah," she asked looking over at me. She moved her bangs out of her face revealing a sensible French tipped manicure. I took a better gander at her hair and determined it was NOT a weave.

"Oh my fault, this is my babes! This is Jason. You've heard me talk about him before with your mama. We havin' a make-up date night," he said smiling all big. She gave me a hug and a kiss on my cheek. "Well damn, this is my niece Donna, you over there making out with."

"Oooo Uncle, he is so phyne. Jason, it's so nice to meet you! Your skin so soft," she said rubbing my arm. Uncle you gotta bring him to TeeTee's birthday and um Mama's barbeque next weekend! It's on Saturday at three. BYOB. Jason, make sure he come, please, 'cause he'll get real bogus and brand new and be all like, ahh baby girl, I forgot, or boo, oh I had to work, or something lame like that," she said batting her long pretty lashes at me.

"I will see what I can do," I smiled trying not to laugh. She was too much.

"Hmm. Okay, cool. Well y'all know what you want?" she asked looking at Gary with her hands on her right hip. She was cheesing like she knew his order.

"Just bring us some wings and fries and two half and halfs," Gary laughed. He looked over at me and winked again. I blushed.

"Ain't nothing changed," she laughed. "Cool, two Gary specials. I got you. The macaroni and cheese is *fyre* today. Spanky ass in the kitchen tonight, boo. So I'm gone bring y'all some," she said turning around and walking off. She rushed back over and hugged Gary again and told me it was nice to meet me before running off to put our order in.

"Twice. Oh, so we just makin' up, now? This how we do that?" I asked with a smirk. Gary just looked at me with them eyes and that smile that got me the first time, nodding his slow cocky *Hell yeah*. I blushed and changed the subject. "She's cute. So what's her story?" I asked taking a biscuit from the basket.

"That's Wanda's husband's daughter from a girl he messed with when he was in college. She got into a little trouble chasing behind some knucklehead who got her pregnant and almost got her disowned from her family. Fool, had her doing some crazy shit for him, babes," he said grabbing a biscuit and taking a bite.

CAY

"Dang, for real?" I said, waiting to hear the rest as I smeared honey butter on a biscuit half.

"Wanda's husband comes from old money, you know. A bunch of snooty mu'fucka's out in the West burbs who treated that little girl like she wasn't shit, babes. Dwight even turned his back on her for a minute. But I talked to him and helped straighten some shit out for her. I check in on her from time to time. She's a good girl, getting her GED, thinking about what she wants to study in college. She do all she can for her little baby boy. She just needs support that's all," Gary said looking over at her at the register ringing up a customer. "So my pops is cool with the owner and we got her this lil' gig here since she basically stay around the corner from here with her moms. Plus she on a train line and can get back and forth to school and her hours don't really affect her study time. She make it work."

"That's what's up, Gary," I said looking at him proudly. I always admired how he asserted his rightful place in his family's lives even in the uncomfortable situations.

I started to come out of my daydream thinking about what was expected of me. I didn't have long before I'd have to say my final best goodbye. I really couldn't pen down a way to articulate everything going on in my head about this tradition I was going to participate in. Mama Larrieux only explained that it was customary for the person they were involved with to say something from the heart on the day of release. She claims it will be cleansing for me, and maybe it will be. I listened to what she had to say as we drove off of the ferry onto dry land.

The route we took was very scenic. It took us fifteen minutes to drive into what looked like a compound of bright colored sturdy concrete houses with an astonishing view of the ocean. The sun was just starting to make its descent as Timothy parked the car in front of a deep bronze colored house. I opened the door and Batman ran out after Porgy and Bess who were outside with Gary's dad Waddie, and Gary's three nephews. I walked up and embraced him while Timothy brought my things into the house. Mama Larrieux kissed her husband and gave him a firm hug.

Gary said to me one time, *I want God to make me his beach. Where everything new in the world comes to me...* I passed it off as just another one of his arrogant quotes. The sight of the cruise ships and the tourists I saw earlier lining the streets as the islands prepared to celebrate their Independence Day - July 10th - put things in a different perspective. This was the first time the outside world invited me to freely express the love I had for one of its own. Without fear for the first time, I recognized I was actually growing up...

SEE

My momma said, this one time, Michael, baby, you know you growin' up when you can get your conscious mind to look at life through your spiritual eyes. *You can see life from both sides of the truth.* Now, when she said that, I wasn't trying to hear it. It was one of them Sundays I was all churched out and we had finished another argument about me going into the Navy. She was like she could pay for me to go to college, or I could take out some student loans and work. It was her churchy way of saying look at other options. I was trying to show Momma, *I gotta spread my wings, nah, come on.* I ain't won't no loans to repay and I ain't want her working triple shifts to take care of no grown ass man. Son or no son.

I graduated high school early and begged her all summer to sign the form to say she gave me permission to join at seventeen. She wasn't having it. So since she was always repeating what the pastor had said to me and my daddy, I had a little chat with him. I scheduled a meeting and everything and presented my case to him and my momma on my computer through this bomb ass PowerPoint presentation. She was in tears before I clicked over to my last slide. She hugged me, signed my lil' form, and had our pastor to pray over me and my decision. He ain't even havta' say nothin'. She saw a grown man that day, I guess. And I saw my mama differently that day. It was a whole other level of caring love. It was like she was testing me and needed to see me make a grown man decision with the reasons behind it to show her hard work as my momma paid off.

I just wanted to join the damn Navy, shit! I asked her why she was crying, and she said the slide that talked about me wanting to be a part of an organization that doesn't see my color only what I can do for it, was the slide that made her give in. She said she never knew just how much of an outsider in the family I felt like. My mama did everything for me. My daddy too, but she didn't have too. She could have given my half-breed ass up for adoption, but she made the grown-up decision to grab hold of what may have been her last chance of motherhood. She was at every one of my football games growing up. She was the loudest momma in the stands. Momma said the part of *her* that she saw in me made her love *the part* she didn't know. And I'm glad I got the chance to know her love.

I took Corey down with me to my family reunion in Covington, Georgia. Almost forty damn miles outside the black gay jungle gym known as Atlanta. All the booty in the world is there this weekend even though the fourth of July was this past Thursday. They still partying, but I ain't thinking about no other booty than Corey's. We may hit up some grind later tonight, though. I done brought sand to the beach. I'm checking my forehead as we speak, and I can say I'm not runnin' a fever.

But wakin' up to somebody I can call *bae* is lookin' kinda' a'ight. Corey is about a couple inches taller than me and I like that. He got them thick cakes and thighs, or hams as I like to call them. He got the pretty dark skin from head to toe, oooooh and dis nigga know he got'sum pretty feet, shit yeah! I can't wait to suck them bad boys while I'm knee deep in it. He got these nice brown lips, with a pink center and dark brown eyes with all this curly ass wild hair. I love this dude and I don't know how he worked his magic on me! I'd see him when I pass by the pharmacy at the Naval Hospital every day just to get a peek at him, once I finally noticed he was alive. But I ain't ever had time to stop. So I'd just slow my stride down and stare at him.

I was looking at him sleeping in my arms when the AC in our hotel room kicked on. I kissed his cheek and sat up a little in bed keepin' my arm around him. He got closer to me, squeezed me tighter, and started snoring a little bit. The shit is cute to me and got me to think about the time I actually saw him up close. I had to get my refill of stay in the world pills. Normally I get them shits during the lunch hour because it's busy and ain't nobody all up in your business. This particular day I was hoping he won't gon' be there and call my number, cause then he'd know my business. I ended up getting called to assist in a code blue, so I would have to try later.

I was on duty that same night. I remember takin' my ass down there being the only one who needed a script. Won't no need to pull a number first to sit down. Nope! I walked up just knowing Corey wouldn't be there and sure as the sky is bright where God live, here he come grinnin' with that pretty dark skin saying he saw me earlier, then asked me how my day went first and foremost. That really stood out to me. Because he looked me in the eye and waited for me to say somethin'. He cared about my day, and that made me feel good. I tried to put my game face on, but his phyne ass was makin' that shit real hard smiling at me. He was definitely a beautiful black man. When I answered him, he complimented me on my deep raspy voice he be trying to imitate now, Georgia drawl and all when I get into my feeling's.

Then, he had these hairy arms with his sleeves cuffed like my boy Jason be doing his shirts. He had the collar starched and both the shirt and them pants hit that body in all the right places for me. With all that curly loose hair. Damn. I sniff his hair all the time. He even had a nice clean shoe. I remember how particular Jason is about his shoes. He'd be like; *a bottom that takes care of his shoes will take care of his man. The shoe gets the most abuse out of anything we put on our bodies. So does a black man...MESSAGE!* Corey is a sneaker hound just like

Jason. But that shit was another check for me. I was like look at my little brother teaching his big bro what to look out fo'.

I like a good old rugged bottom, and Corey is the opposite of that even though he from Chicago. He's soft though and has this nurturing side that lets his inner sissy play hide and seek with his masculine appearance. It's cool to me to sit there and watch him discover and interact with people and the world. He's opened my eyes to a whole lot of shit I ain't never thought about. I was happy with going back to my lil' life inside the 285 bubble. I guess like Jason, he showing me that its shit beyond the perimeter, you jus' gotta go for it.

It's gon' be interestin' when him and Jason do meet. Jason ain't never liked none of the dates I messed with. Like this one time, I remember I didn't have time to drop Jason off before I went to go pick up one of my bust down's. The original plan was to pick this nigga up from the south side and put his ass on the train in Great Lakes when Spike was satisfied. But this time me and Jason was comin' from this lil' grind out in Jolliet, and the date text my phone sayin', he was ready. Well I ain't feel like ridin' all the way up north to drop Jason off to haf'ta come back, so we stopped and got him and wouldn't you know, Jason ass gotta piss.

I tell my date to let him use his bathroom and shit and he invites us up. It looked like he had just straightened the place up before he buzzed us up. Jason walks in the bathroom and walks right back out a few seconds later, with this look on his face that had me concerned. I was like, *you pissed that fast Jay,* and my boy was like *Mike, I'll hol'it till you drop me at home.* I was like damn! The date came out of the kitchen and we all got cozy in the Bootillac listenin' to that gutta.

Jason in the back seat sendin' me texts and shit. I'm reading this shit with the date next to me dyin'. I'm trying to hold my laughs in. Jason was like Mike, *A triflin' bathroom makes a triflin' bottom, you've been warned.* In my mind I was thinking, I ain't need to read that bull jive right now, Jason! Damn! I looked over at my date and slapped his thigh and was like, *my man, we ain't gon' have NO problems tonight, are we?* I asked inquiring about his plumbing situation. Jason stupid ass started cracking up when the boy confidently said, *Oh, I'm good.* Sure as shit stinks, dude painted all over my brand-new Polo sheets less than five minutes into my initial deep stroke game. He was a *nice* chocolate boy too! I just knew that ass was gon' be right. But he couldn't handle the dick anyway. He was one of them Boyz II Men bottoms. Talm'bout, ooh ahh, oooohh aahhh ouch stop wait type nigga's. I immediately put that ass on a south bound train.

I didn't know what wait, meant, until Corey. He the first guy that's made me *wait.* I actually have to date Corey the old-fashioned way. This game of cat and mouse as my daddy say, is sexy as shit to me. I see why them fool's was fighting over Jason. I got a few more tests to run befo' I let him challenge Jason. But if he get the little bro's stamp of approval, he may be sum'n to hol'on too. I'm sure he'd agree with what my momma used to say when she'd tell me to stop runnin' my way through life.

Corey is HIV positive too so he understands the struggle and can relate to the fact that I'm fast approaching thirty and been living with this shit my whole life. He understands me when I say I'm scared that I won't have time to run out and challenge all of lifes thrills. He understands me when I say I'm tired physically, but I force myself not to be. So while I still have the energy and the mind set to do and see every thang I can outside of my own personal 285, I'm gon' do it. I got somebody I feel like I can do that stuff with now, because they understand my need for living like I ain't gon' see tomorrow.

The thought of a calendar stresses me out. Calendars put a number on my days that forever reminds me of how many days and years I've lived with this shit and the stress of wondering how many more of them fucker's I have left. Time stresses me out. Momma used to tell me start enjoying the things in front of you that you pass by every day, because you'll notice something new each and every time. She said even if it's just a hole in the wall or a crack in the pavement. She said always look for something new to see. She said, *God never does any one thing the same. No one germ is like the other exactly and no one hair on your head is the same either, baby. So always look for the new thing God wants to give you. Meaning, what else has God done?* That was after she felt I was old enough to stop tellin' me that my HIV was a secret medical *thangy* that only the two of us shared.

I was a lil' boy then. My ears would perk up when I heard anything AIDS/HIV related after that. Cause this conversation now involved me and my momma. So shit yeah, I needed to know what was hap'nin. But I remember thinking that I was gon' die because I had these microscopic bugs in me that I couldn't squash with my gym shoes. It's crazy after all this time, its stuff to kill every bug and germ in the world except HIV/AIDS. It's like being stuck with them two ig'nant ass kin I got, that just won't get a clue when I tell'em jus cause I sneeze that don't mean I'm dying or you gon' "catch" it.

When I had to get on meds, I was scared to death. Up until then, it was like I didn't have it. Momma cried with me on the phone the day Jason came over to check on me. She demanded that I wake him up so that she could thank him for being there with me. They had to have talked about an hour in the other room. Knowing her she told him to step away from me. Till this day I'oughnt know what she said to him, but he came out the room like he had been crying. Momma must have used that gift she had, so I know she gave him what he needed.

SEE

Every time I called and talked to her, she'd always ask about Jason. And tell Jason this and tell Jason that. And I'd just nod and smile and say yes ma'am and be flipping Jason's uppity black ass off at the same time. He'd hear her on the phone and they ass would be talkin' with me caught in the middle of they conversation. But that's just how momma was. I used to love going home for Mother's Day. She'd always act surprised to see me and kiss and cry all on me like she ain't seen me in years. I'd be like, *momma I was jus' down here a couple months ago*. And she'd rush off to the Farmers Market to get fresh peaches to make me a cobbler. I wish she could have met Jason in person, but it never seemed to pan out.

I could share with my momma how I was feelin' when I was having one of my days where the medication would have my stomach in knots from bein' constipated. When my levels would improve, she understood what that meant. She gave me diet tips when my doctors had to switch one of my meds because it was spiking my cholesterol. Little things like that I could talk to her about, because we were the only two in the family who had the medical "thangy". We would share the latest things we learned and sit on the phone sometimes watchin' news specials on it. I didn't know nobody I was going to be able to really be free to talk to about that type of stuff with until I met Corey.

SEE

That night at the pharmacy, he came back to the counter with my meds. My mouth was dry. My heart was pounding out my chest. I was nervous as shit. He pointed to one of the bottles before putting it in a paper bag and said, *this one right here makes me burp the first hour of taking it. Yuck!* I laughed and told him it did the same thing to me *Drink a little warm water behind it.* After that, our eyes talked about sumthin' on their own and then, so did we. I don't even feel out of character, none of my fuck boy shit, just something new, out da blue. Thanks, Momma, for teaching me what to see...

GEE

"Waddie, tell him make sure that the boat is goin' against the wind dear," Gary's mom yelled up to her husband who was talking to the captain of the yacht. The family rented it for Gary's send off as well as the parents' retirement party. Mama Larrieux wanted to combine the two, so the occasion could be shared with the spirit of her oldest boy in tow.

"Wo'mun, what you worried for, ay? Ya skeered to get bone bits on ya. Them bones come from us, ya know?" Gary's dad yelled back down laughing as the captain smiled and slapped him on the back. He blew out a puff of smoke.

"Waddie, I just don't want nothing blowing in my face now. I don't wunna taste Gary's bone, maybe Jason does, but not me," she said laughing and giving me a firm side hug. I laughed at how these two were making me the butt of their gay jokes the same as when it was both Gary and me.

"How 'bout it Jay'sun, you wunt Gary's bone in ya' little peach fuzz ya growin' dere mun?" Mr. Larrieux asked before laughing. I gagged and looked at Mrs. Larrieux.

"Sprinkle mine over some sorbet, and feed it to me," I teased as Mr. Larrieux cracked up.

"You two are horrible, I'm goin' to check on the boys," Mama Larrieux said laughing and letting me go. Some of my nerves dissipated. "Down wind, please driver! Boat mover or captain. Whatever, you are!" she said laughing and walking away.

"I make sure we downwind, ma'am!" The captain said smiling and waving at her, letting out another puff of smoke.

I was pretty anxious as we made our way off the coast of the island of Exuma. I walked through the crowd of family and introduced myself. Some knew who I was and walked up to me telling me that Audry, Gary's mother, had been bragging about me writing this amazing poem to honor her beloved son. That only raised my level of anxiety. I hoped I lived up to the hype that Mama Larrieux stirred up.

I must have combed through those words a million times. I wrote the piece onto a scroll I planned to give to Gary's parents with a frame that I bought soon after committing to do this. I'm going to give it to them as one of their retirement gifts from our household. Gary and I got them season courtside seats to watch their favorite team - the Miami Heat. They were both die-hard basketball fans and Gary and his dad would play with Timothy and his friend from the West side from time to time.

I really needed to live up to the hype. I looked around and saw a family of proud black men and women, direct descendants of freed Black people now on their own land inherently handed over to them by the British. The women in Gary's family were exquisite, regal, and strong. All of them wore their own beautiful head of natural hair. Some had their hair braided, others locked, or straighten, low and kinky, or set in long soft coils. I mean, these were stunning beautiful black women who didn't feel a need to sow another woman's DNA into their scalps to feel lovely. I haven't seen black women this natural since the 90's.

I remember when I was little, I asked Granny why our hair was the way it was. She told me that God knew we were going to go through the hard times of slavery, so he prepared us to be a strong spiritual people with thick curly course hair that we could comfortably relax our tired heads on because in the days of slavery, there weren't such things as the pillows we have today. Granny was like, *Thank God that you have a strong yet comfortable head of hair like Sampson. Black people have so much strength in us that it finds its way into our hair. That's why they're scared of it. You can do and be anything you want as a black man and so can your hair.* She loved when I grew a high-top fade in my early teens. The men were tall, handsome, and rugged men's men. Like my dad, they commanded respect in the gentle proud manner that black men of standards possess.

I wandered around, people watching, and reciting the poem in my head. I wanted to make sure I knew each line by heart. I didn't want to stumble. I didn't want to have to repeat a messed-up syllable. I had to be on point. I didn't have time to really focus on my own feelings because I didn't feel it was about me. I was here and this was for Gary. Gary's sister Adrienne grabbed my hand laughing disturbing the personal recital of my prose.

"Jason, you've got to come hear this! You know my cousin Althea I was telling you about yesterday?" she asked with this huge smile on her face. "She was telling me how she think no one knows she been messing with this guy on the island named Clyde who all the women wanted, but he only has eyes for her." Adrienne reiterated how she carries on like she doesn't care about him, but behind closed doors and around the women in the family, it's a very different story. I shook my head yes, letting her know I remembered what she told me. "Well she's talking about him now. Come quick and have a listen," she said whisking me off to the where Althea was talking to another one of their cousins.

"So what it's rainin' ot'side. I don't hafto worry 'bout no hair no more. Me cut it shart for me no mess with it lung time before werk! He gon' pull up here looking big and swole or som'n in the car in front of av'ree wun dere! Gun tuuurn his window don' tell'un me get it in the car, no! I say g'won dere now boy bringin' foolishness round 'bout me now! Hear what I say, g'won den now!"

"Why not just get in the car Thea? Why you runnin' the man away now, he's only trying his luck with takin' ya, on the town." One of the cousins stated. Adrienne held her tongue and me tight as she was getting a kick out of this.

"Safi, I a strung wo'mun, ya know. I don't know why I need a man to fight battles for me. Oh he just made me mad so dem so. I was just cross about'a bus dat t'rove by splashing mud on my new dress, ya know! I tell'em, why you no come with the car before the bus come splashin' at me, ay?" She said, explaining how she scorned this mystery man willing to put up with this shrew.

"Thea how he gon' know about a bus? He was trying to rescue you," Safi said laughing. I smiled and nodded in agreement.

"The point Safi is, he just should have come to my aid sooner. I was upset, ya know, den em stick an umba'rella t'rew the win'dow. I say to'em, just like a man, ya see me got all'a dem bags here boy! Ya wun give me som'n more to carry up the road dere now? The woes men give ya," Adrienne burst into laughter. Safi stood there with her eyes closed shaking her head. She was looking up at the sky and sighed heavily.

"When ya seein' him again Althea?" Safi said shaking her head again. She smiled, rolled her eyes, and focused her attention on Althea.

"I seein' em on Tuues'dee!" Althea said quickly blushing and covering her mouth like a little schoolgirl. Althea looked at me and Adrienne smiling at one another.

"So why you stop from getting' in the car with him yu' crazy cow?!" Safi asked in undeniable frustration.

"Because I was not too far from home! Soakin' wet already, dere was nooo point to wet his seats Safi," Althea said as I chuckled.

"What you laughing for dere, Jay'sun? What you got ta' stick up the men for?" she said putting her hands on her hip waiting for my reply with pursed lips.

"Gary used to do simple nice stuff like that for me all the time. He'd do what he could to either fix or help fix my problems. I would do the same for him. That's what real men do. With all the crap that comes against us as black men, it's nice to have a chance to be able to come against...*something*. Anything. And be a hero. Whoever this man is, you need to let him grab hold of you. You'll miss it when it's gone. When it stops, when he stops. You need to remember men don't have the same patience as God. Excuse me, ladies," I said smiling politely before walking away. That heffa is the reason they say chivalry is dead.

I wished I could go and check on my dog, but he was at the house. I felt like I needed to throw up. I found a part of the yacht that wasn't occupied with silly people and took a big gulp of sea air and held on to it until I became lightheaded. I braced myself against the rail. A glimpse of the family appeared in my peripheral, bountifully clad in white linen, island style. We all had a green flower pinned to us to honor Gary. Green was his favorite color. I turned to face forward again and closed my eyes, getting carried away with the up and down list of the bow. I was able to recite the whole poem in its entirety twice before I felt a firm hand on my shoulder. When I opened my eyes and looked to my right, Gary's father offered me his handsome smile as he lit his cigar. I saw traces of his son in his posture.

"Jason, I know my son will neva get to 'ear me say dis to you, but...the mo'mant I lay eyes upon ya dere with my boy, I saw a great per'sun...for my boy." He took a long pull from his cigar, which I realized was a spliff. He looked out towards the water. He leaned over the side slightly and spit. "I apologize to ya for yur loss, ya know. I neva say dat to ya before. I had my ways about me, ya know. Not a thing against you. Jus' my child, my ol'dest boy was gone. Killed you know. If I felt how, I felt, I knew you felt sum'thin terrible in yur rib too. I shuud have talk to ya bout dat be'fore long," he smiled slightly and looked at me with sorrow and palpable sympathy I could feel.

He handed me the spliff and watched me hesitantly take it into my grasp. I recalled what Dee had taught me and took a couple of pulls. We took in the moment enjoying the relaxing sound of the water under the vessel. The breeze massaged my heightened sensitivity as the effects took hold. I broke the silence.

"Mr. Larrieux. You know, he shielded...me...and..." I tried to speak, but I lost it. I collapsed. Mr. Larrieux caught me, and I cried like a baby in his arms. "I'm sorry, Mr. Larrieux, this hurts so much...this hurts me so deep, sir."

"Let it out, son. It's okay to do so dere boy. You go'wun dere and fret so. Those ar' tears of luv," he said.

"I feel responsible, and I'm sorry," I confessed.

"It's not yur fault. Don't take on dat dere. You must rejoice in da luv you two shared. Let it go son, it's all right dere now, boy," Mr. Larrieux said rubbing my back. "Ya finally let him go. He can keep watchin' o'va you now from heaven, ya freed him, dere now," he said, reaching into his shirt pocket to hand me a handkerchief. I cleaned my face up and got my scene together. He walked me down to the fantail of the yacht and stood me in front of everyone. He gave me a hug and took the urn from Mama Larrieux.

The immediate family stood behind me, his mother, Wanda his oldest sister, his younger sister Adrienne, and the baby brother Timothy. Gary's father poured ashes into the hand of each family member behind me. I held back my tears as best I could when I felt the cool course fragments of my partner in my hands for the first time. Gary's dad whispered that he was proud of me. I gripped his remains tightly in my hand and closed my eyes as Mr. Larrieux prayed over the ceremony. I'll be glad when life finally gives me something back. I actually said in my head as he prayed. I don't know if that's a selfish statement or not, but that's how I felt.

I thought about how I hadn't been to church in a long time. The islanders hold religion and spirituality in high regard just like many other people of African descent. It amazes me that we as a black people are scattered all over the globe and are uniquely and universally all wired to be in tune and tap into our spiritual side without fail. This trip so far has shown me a different side of God that I had been told my whole life I'd never see because I was gay.

For the first time in my life, I'm living for me. I'm discovering my talents; I'm feeling young again. I'm not in hiding and I'm not on the run anymore. Today wasn't easy for me, especially now that I am grasping the dust he left behind. I found the courage to stand strong with his family and vocalize these words I simply call, Gee:

Lust is a sure thing,
But Love requires a little courting.
Its agenda has no time or date to bloom,
It's an impromptu kiss you don't have to ask for,
Just connect,
Green lights given become reckless when the currency for the same established high becomes unbridled.
Lust has the equivalent time stamp of the suns unavoidably ignored race across the sky,

Love looks like the sun,

Warmth and exuberant brilliance that you cannot stare into,

It's too bright a shine.

Love takes leisurely steps for a slow steady race,

Not the galloping face of a hallmark farmer with red roses and babies breath.

Lust is a quick pick me up,

Encouragement however slight,

But you can't fall in love with a sound bite,

No,

Not when there is an embrace like this that I get to scoot into as we tuck away from the stress I tenderly removed from your temples and shoulders.

Your feet.

You were more than a just for me,

But a must for me,

Thanking God He placed someone extraordinary,

And in enough love with me to finally step forward.

Someone brave enough to stare into my sunlight,

Man enough to assert his primitive instinct to protect me on Earth one last night.

I can't believe I found the words to proclaim my love,

Pay my final respects,

Kiss both of your wings,

And muster up the strength to let this final visible piece of love from you,

GEE

Fly,
In many directions I leave fragments of Gee,
Letting the love in my eyes trust the wind I cannot see,
Taking a moment to reflect with a selfish pardon,
To sift the beauty in your ashes through my fingers,
So that Love can replenish her garden.

JAY

"Jason's name keeps coming up in a lot of your sessions, Westbrook? What was your relationship with this young man?" CDR Jamison asked. He leaned back in his big comfy ass chair and gave me this smirk. He tried to cover it up, but I saw it.

"You trying to add sodomy charges to my rap sheet doc?" I asked looking at him like all of a sudden I couldn't care less.

"Would that matter to you?" he retorted.

"Shit, probably not." I said.

"No, Westbrook. I'm simply trying to see where he resides in your life. His significance to you can help me find answers and ask the right questions to help me to help you," he said pointing at me with that professionally trained reassuring smile of his. I sized him up.

"I'm only talkin' today 'cause I feel like...I'm just saying, sir, it just seemed like you were judging me," I said trying to respect his crooked ass collar device. *He didn't see that shit this morning, or when he went to the bathroom, or grabbed lunch?* That shit was driving me crazy. *Why is his service corps insignia crooked?! WHY DO I CARE?!*

I tried focusing on something else, shit. A pen, a thumbtack, fuck, one of the many dead roaches I seen lying on its back up in here this week after they fumigated. I ain't ever know what a roach was until I got in here. *Who the fuck lives with roaches?* But my eyes stayed locked and loaded on this disgrace of a Navy uniform. Here I am in polished boots and pressed orange coveralls more squared away than this fool sitting here judging me. I'm even sporting military creases! I might be able to tolerate the coffee stain, though. Call it the shit I learned in Officer's sensitivity bullshit ass training.

"I'm not judging you and I apologize to you for giving you that impression. No harm no foul...?" he asked. I didn't even look at his face.

"Jason has a...CDR Jamison," I stopped, closed my eyes, and looked back at his crooked insignia. I couldn't continue to ignore it. I personally knew men who died in that uniform. "Can you please fix your collar device, its distracting me, sir?" He looked at me and nodded his head. Here I was a decorated convict correcting a fucking senior officer who was supposed to be rehabilitating me and he can't respect the uniform enough to stay squared away in front of a junior officer. Former or not. I hate when these PhD entitlement seeking assholes disrespect the uniform. I tried to chill out, but the shit really irked me.

"I didn't know it was disturbed, pardon me shipmate," he said while he looked down and adjusted it. "Is that better?" I didn't answer I just continued my story. I was trying to keep it together, so that he wouldn't detect I wasn't taking those pills he took upon himself to prescribe.

"Jason is gay," I said laughing as a thought of Jason leaving caused me to look out of the window. It was very sunny outside making me miss the smell of fresh air. My laughter and smile disappeared. "Jay was my diary. I could talk to him about whatever and he'd always have an answer for me. I poured my guts out to him. I never thought he'd close the book on me."

"So, he was a confidant more or less?" CDR asked for clarification. He wrote something down on his pad really quick and looked back up at me.

"He's something more than that," I said trying to figure out how much I was going to tell him. "Can you turn some of these lights off, sir?"

"So, you care a great deal about him?" he said getting up to adjust the lights. He then crashed back down into that big ass chair.

"I do, and it's just not right...him...hey this is pissing me off. Can we change the topic? I don't know if I want to talk...I'm sorry doc, I just don't..." I said trying to control my breathing.

"Westbrook, that's fine. This is your session. It's alright, brotha, relax and breathe in through your nose and out through your mouth," he said moving in closer. He took his glasses off and sat them on his desk. He placed both of his hands on his desk and elongated his torso to start breathing with me. Somehow it made me feel better and after stepping in this office for a year, I finally felt like he was with me. After a few cycles, I guess he noticed I calmed down, and he started talking again. "Why don't you start from the beginning? Why didn't you and your father ever bring any fish home? That was the last thing you expressed the other week." He leaned back and looked me in the eyes. There was no barrier between his eyes and mine. He kept his glasses off and on his desk. He had finally gained my trust.

"It was only one day I remember we didn't bring any fish home. That was when Dad bust in on us, finally..." I said pausing and slouching down in my seat, still holding his gaze. I scratched my head and the sound of the chain scared the shit out of me causing me to flinch. It's an irritating sound I still can't get used too.

"Are you okay, Westbrook?" CDR Jamison asked. I just continued without bringing more attention to myself. I probably did need those pills, but I didn't like them.

"Dad loved giving me any and everything I wanted. He was very generous. Sometimes too much in my opinion but he didn't mind sharing the fruits of his labor. He said it kept him humbled and grounded that he had what we needed even if we didn't need it. It made him feel like the good man MiMi said my Grandpop was. He said he did it out of love...love...I didn't know the meaning of that word until I looked back over the years that my dad was there for me and how he graciously and humbly lives his life," I said looking at doc with tears in my eyes. I just let them fall. CDR kept a compassionate eye on me. "Dad was always there for me man, even when I didn't know it. He knew about me and he protected me. But I hated that shit...this thing inside of me because of Uncle Richard. Doc, he was my dad's older fucked up in the head ass brother. Dad would bail him out, give him money, put his credit and name on the line, for this mutha'fucka to turn around and lay up in my bed the night before our big fly-fishing trip to Florida. I was so fuckin' excited," I smiled still letting my tears flow. I looked down at my hands and then up at the ceiling. He was so rough with me man, and I couldn't move. I was like ninety-five pounds man. I was a fuckin' kid and this nigga, that piece of shit that my dad rescued time and time again and loved unconditionally, fucked me like I was one of his cell mates..." I took some time to gather my thoughts.

"Take your time, sir, and breathe," CDR instructed.

"He was humming some...some song in my ear that I couldn't figure out the whole time he was fuckin' me. I was trying my damnedest to scream or break free, but that big mutha'fucka kept holding me down grunting and humming. And, and, and, and sweatin' his low class sweat on me. I kept thinking was this punishment for having those thoughts they tell you are wrong? Is this the sign telling me that I need to think about this shit a little deeper? I didn't get the chance to figure this shit out for myself like Jason did. It was forced on me. I didn't...have...the opportunity to consult God about what was going on. All I know is I wasn't going to be like my Uncle Richards bum ass," I said as tears began to really flow. I had to let this shit go. It was about time.

"Do you need a break, Westbrook?" CDR Jamison asked handing me some tissues. I took a few and wiped my face. I looked at him and shook my head no, blowing my nose. I balled the tissue up and chucked it into the wastebasket like I was on the basketball court. I took a deep breath and kept talking.

"I wanted to KILL that nigga! I didn't understand why he did that to me, man, it was all good earlier riding around in his Iroc-Z and then...man...this is crazy. I thought I was over that shit man. I thought I was over it. I'm grown now man, so why does it even matter? I don't know why I did it, but I wrote Jason...seventeen letters of open apologies for the way I treated him, and about the way I handled...sex...the way I handled him when I was...sexin' him. I did him the same way my Uncle did me because I thought that was how you...two men have sex. He didn't deserve that...to be fucked and then fucked over by me and then I find out that same night his ex-boyfriend rapes him for real. I just...could have prev...I should have stopped it. And I guess that's why I don't care that I killed him. I never want that to happen to someone I love again. I just wanted Jay to know that. That low life don't deserve...he didn't deserve no man like Jason," I scoffed.

"Jason is the only person whose heart I didn't have to bribe my way into. And I tried to do it anyway. I'm a confused man..." I hung my head down and tried to grab a hold of my mind. I was starting to slip. I kept telling myself to chill out and slow down.

I thought back to the night Jason laid up with me in a little bungalow I rented at Onslow Beach. This was back when we were both stationed at Camp Lejeune, North Carolina. It was the same day we went running on the sand. Just a lazy ass day afterwards. He wanted carbs, so we went and got waffles and came back to the spot and crashed. I remember how good and edible he smelled to me. Them gay feelings I used to have started to creep up on me.

There was only one full size bed in the room, so our two big grown asses climbed in and before I realized it, he was nestled right up on me. My dick got hard and scared the shit out of me. But that was the most peaceful night of sleep I ever had. Whenever I'd sleep like that next to Jay, I knew everything was cool. I fell hard for him. I felt like that was my, boo. But I wasn't supposed to love him like that, because I didn't want to let that part of me grow. That shit felt so correct, that I couldn't help but keep tabs on him. I kept telling myself, revisit this later. *Revisit this later.* I wasn't ready to deal with it. *Revisit this later.* This wasn't right when Cindy was still on my line and hoes was coming across my sheets on a regular. *Revisit this later.*

So my future wife was bound to take her rightful place, or so I thought.

I graduated top of my class from Howard University, too dumb to factor in the obvious. He was so right for me and I was probably so right for him. He obviously knew this shit all along, staying diligent the entire time we could see each other freely, face to face, without chains and starched orange coveralls restricting the touch from someone you care so fuckin' much for but was too much of a coward to show. I'd leave too if it was him who only pops up in my life when it's convenient.

I treated him as an expendable good and for that I'm the one who should even feel lucky he respected me enough to tell me point blank to my face, *yo, no hard feelings, but I didn't read your letters, bruh.* He definitely can't keep waiting now. That man has to live his life and I can respect that. I got my own shit to work out too, so...I'm back to primitive status. Waiting on snail mail like it's cool. No Internet here. I am off the grid. Today, I got a letter from MiMi telling me what dad said before my hearing. I had asked her about it in my last letter to her. She said he couldn't bare to come inside the actual court room to see them auction off his son to both the state and federal government. The first letter he wrote since I was sentenced came today. I can't open it yet. I'll open it when I feel the time is right. MiMi said he may not have been in there, but he was just behind the doors supporting me with humble dignity.

I imagined him busting into the courtroom saving his son from the arm of the law just like the night he burst into my bedroom and choke slammed Uncle Richard to the ground knocking him out for the count. Dad hogtied and strapped that mutha'fucka to the banister and wrapped me in a blanket to rush me to the hospital. He called the police and they hauled that fool away. I don't know what I am because I suppressed a lot of me. Without me knowing it, Dad made a pallet in my room and slept guarding me like a hawk for a while after it happened. I didn't realize it until I woke up to piss one night. I felt like he knew. Because that wasn't the first time Uncle Richard tried me. A bedroom only tells half the story with the light off...

DEE

Jason,

I'm about to come clean with you about a lot of things in these letters to you. When I saw you at my hearing, I knew you had made me your enemy even though you had every right to do so. I was like, I hope it's not to late because I owe you more than an explanation. I owe you the truth even if I lose you for good.

I know you may think you have me all figured out, but I'm writing to tell you that you don't know me at all. You know shards of who I am. Lately, the mirror reflects a broken man. I'm so made up I don't even know me anymore. Shit, I fucking shot your boyfriend, so yeah, something ain't right.

You only know my representative, Jay. That's what I've been raised to be. I've been groomed to put on airs for years. Some things I've told you were half-truths I was trying to be brave and just tell you about. I wanted to blurt out who I was to you so many times before, knowing I could trust you. I knew you wouldn't judge me or force me to do something I didn't want to do. I've been forced to do shit my whole life, Jason. Even killing your guy. I wish I had the courage you did to just, rebel and go against who they tell you to be. I don't have nothing but time on my hands to spill my shit to you, so here goes.

JAY

I've been my dad's puppet my whole fucking life. I was just another one of his trophies to show off like Mama's prized chocolate and bronze poodles. I was an accomplishment in upper crust black society. I came from good stock, proud well to do people of color who were only concerned with the aesthetics of things. Surface people, who I call, surface clowns, whose idea of being deep was to throw money at any issue below the surface of their feet.

I was told what to wear, what to say, who to talk too, don't be too black, but be black, but don't be "that" black. Be "this much" black. My dad got whatever he wanted and made sure I did as well. But it all came at a cost. He was driven, well respected, the top of his class, the top of his grade, the top of his profession, highly decorated, and received a lot of his clout after performing two delicate procedures for the POTUS. I could go on and on about his accolades, but he still was empty inside. He had us as a family and nice homes and wealth and was still unfulfilled. He was living a lie, like me.

It pains me to ask how I can be in love with you and feel that it's wrong. You are the most beautiful thing I have left in this world and I messed that up. I apologize for taking that away from you in your own form. I wish you something greater than what I inadvertently took away from you baby boy. I cannot change what I've done; I cannot rationalize what I've done. I cannot expect you to understand.

All I can say is I told myself I can't be what you want me to be for you, and I knew the day I came to visit you with the flowers that you felt the same. Honestly, now we'll never know if we were wrong because I still love you, man. No one took the time to be there for me like you. You would stop what you were doing to see about me. But I don't want to be gay. This gay thing scares me, man. But you intrigued me. I felt so comfortable with you and so at home with you that I fell in love with you even though I don't agree with two niggas fuckin' around. This whole gay thing was forced on me by my dad's fucked up in the head ass brother. My dad tried hard to escape his reality of being abused by his older brother, so much so that he created this so-called perfect life to somehow magically make that part of his life go away.

When I became a teenager, we would go on these fishing trips and we'd do all kinds of fun shit on the boat and fish and cook and eat, and then Uncle Richard started showing up on our trips. I suppressed all that shit man when he was gone. But when he was in town, it was like my mind would throw up what I was trying to force it to swallow.

My reality was waking up late evening after late evening with Uncle Richard sneaking into my room like the fucking tooth fairy. Dad was gone TDY for a few days.

JAY

I'd feel the wetness of my uncle's tongue on my ass as he readied me for his long-winded release. I'd just lie there toughing through the pain creating a shopping list of things I'd want to do and buy because that's what my dad's guilt of being gone all the time purchased. The sky was the limit and I'd include my little sister in on the treasure trove as well. There were times I'd hurt so bad that I wouldn't eat for a couple days so that I wouldn't have to go to the bathroom.

My dad came back early this time for some reason. It was the same night I felt like this had to stop for good. I was tired of it. The more I fought the more he bore down on me. I tried my damnedest to not be overpowered by him. I was a fucking kid Jason.

My dad and I had a conversation about it after my uncle was sentenced. He told me that he used to do the same thing to him when he was younger. They were twelve years apart in age, and when he came home from a failed attempt at a Naval career, he just wasn't the same. He wasn't happy. He started molesting him at night. My dad told me he wasn't gay, but Uncle Richard was. He fought his brother off one night with a toy car he hid under his pillow. He didn't want me to be like his brother. He thought that's what being gay was. I thought the same thing until I met you, Jason.

But dad apologized for letting that happen to me. Nothing he could do would erase what happened. I testified in court against my uncle. I just wanted to get on with my life and I was determined to show my dad what a real family looked like. I wanted to fix me and my Dad. I was determined to do this shit right. That was my plan. I was all-good. My dad paid for all four years of my education at Howard, and I followed in his footsteps and joined the Navy enlisted and then went the officer route. I was going to do this thing right, man.

But then I met you and all of those confusing feelings I had came up. All the dames I was dicking down were one-dimensional compared to you. You looked at me for me and you were patient. I actually took notice of how you have control of your own world, but you don't realize how big it is. Why is that? You helped me figure out who I was and all I could think to do was treat you like one of my dames, and play on your emotions, and bring you red roses and sit with my feet kicked up on your table like I paid for it. I'm sorry, Jay. I owe you so much more than that. Especially now. You showed me I could trust another man.

The thing is, when I sexed you that night it was like I opened up something I needed to release. I felt like I rough housed you like my uncle did me. Then, I just leave you in your feelings because I didn't feel right about the possibility of us. I'm not gay is what I kept telling myself because I don't want to be, Jason. And then when you told me old boy raped you, I snapped because you are too great a person to be treated like the way me and that nigga treated you. Or how my own blood treated me. I apologize, Jason, and I don't know what that can mean for you, but I am deeply sorry for my part in all this.

When I found out ol' boy dogged you out like that my intention was to go over there and scare him with the gun and get him to confess to raping you, so I could lock his ass away like my piece of shit uncle. But when he lurched towards me trying to cover you, I panicked and shot him. To me he was an enemy. I'm sorry, Jason. I regret that because my intent was not to take a life and destroy another. I pray you forgive me as I search my heart to forgive myself.

MiMi says when you're in your mess and don't deal with it, you'll do things you never thought you were capable of. That's why it's not fair to judge anyone. If you were they, what would you do? Well, if I had it to do all over again, it wouldn't be to kill a man, even though I wanted him to pay for what he did.

I'm afraid. Things didn't turn out like I planned. My perfect family slipped out of my hands the day my baby girl died in my arms. That was one of the saddest days of my life Jay, so I think on some level I may be able to empathize with you. I didn't know how to respond when my dad asked about you and asked me to invite you on a special fishing trip, just the three of us.

JAY

I should have never told him about you. I should have kept you to myself. But maybe that's my problem. I remember you telling me more than once that I can't always get what I want. Try telling that to a boy who has never ever heard no. That's one reason I stayed in the gym so much. No one was going to tell me no, and no one was going to overpower me. But somehow, the feelings I had for you did, and this is the result. And there it is, the truth.

Dee

Jason,

Man, it's been a couple weeks and a nigga look out for a letter from you every time they do mail call. What's up bro? This is week number three in this mug, man. I'm not really ready to talk about this shit, but I will say this. You know how people think the military must be like, yeah, this is it, man. Real talk. Jason, man. I miss my homeboy. I miss you man. I hope you got to read the letter I wrote and can see why I'm so fucked up in the head man. I snapped, man, and I'm sorry Jason. Man, they got me hopped up on this medication shit because I'm depressed from PTSD and shit like that's what the doctor told me man. So I haven't really been saying anything to the doctor, man, because Jay man, you know them

JAY

Psychedelic kats is a bunch of ol' nonsense. You know how I feel about the PhD's. What black person you knew go to see a damn shrink, bruh, you feel me? Yo', you feel me, Jay, I know you do, but yo', they got your boy on these nasty ass pills man, and I wanted to tell you about it because I can't talk to the doctors because you the only one I can talk to man because you know you's my dude, man. I mean, I know if don't nobody else got it you do man, you know my back. I mean you got my back. Shit, I'm writing in a pen, so I can't erase my mistakes so please bear with me, my man, but I'm on this medication and the doctors is askin me these questions about me and how I did and why I did what I did, you know shot that nigga. I'm sorry, Jay, I shot Larry, I'm sorry. If you see him though tell him I'm sorry too. But yo', he asked what happened, and I didn't say shit, but I kept thinking about how I shot him, and you had all that nigga blood on you like it was ketchup and shit. Remember back in the day they said that that was the stuff, ketchup, that that was what the y used to use to make the blood. In scary shows. I always thought that was a lie until I took my medication and saw Larry in your room all bloody and you was trying to give him CPR like how I did Mendez out in the sand box. I pissed on myself Jason when I pulled her body in half, I pissed on myself and I didn't know what the fuck was going on, like death was following me and I felt like that I was like so what if I don't know why. I gotta get home to see my dude. Jason, I wanted to see you again just to tell me that it was going to be alright. I had money and cars and women, shit pussy galore nigga, and trips and college and all kinds of shit man I didn't need. They say don't let your mouth write a check that your ass can't cash, but I guess my mouth and my ass worked very well together because they got me a bunch of empty gift boxes that lost their appeal after the trinket taken out. Man, I don't how I'm complaining when you had to work hard for everything you have even your family and friends, man, shit ain't handed to you, Jay, but I pray that changes for you, man. My time in your life is up and I'm just dead weight anyway and I apologize for dragging you this long, but that's no excuse for me killing that dude you loved, I'm sorry, I'm just feeling myself right now I guess, I would have been a better choice thought if I wasn't straight. You read that in the last letter? I hope you did man, because I think I told you everything you needed to know man, Jason, please write me back man, I miss you, dude. I miss you, man. For real dude, hit your boy back and please send me some lotion that lotion you always send I'm gon' tell the MA to look out for it man. Please I love you dude. Alright.

Dee

Jason,

So, it's been about two months now and I'm guessing I really need to stop counting down the time or I'll make myself go crazy. You remember that's the worst thing you can do in the military, out in the field with the jarheads. This is a combat zone of the mind, because I don't have nothing but time.

So I hope everything is going well on your end, Jay. How are your mom, the family, and Batman doing? How are you doing? That's the most important question I have. I just want to apologize again man and let you know that there isn't a day that goes by that I haven't thought about what I allowed my anger to do. I'd give anything to take that back. I find myself wondering what you're doing and wondering what you would have done if you were me.

I find myself thinking about how you would have handled your emotions, your feelings, your thoughts, and your urges. I mean you were so patient with me man, like you didn't trip on the fact that you had a thing for me but knew I wasn't ready to face my own interpretation.

Shit, Jason, I don't know, man. But what I do know is, I'm sorry. I hope you are reading my letters and can kind of understand how things took a turn for the worst. I think what I was doing was putting more stock into what I wanted to prove rather than into who I was. It's a matter of asking, what's the difference between to believe and to *know? Is to believe disrespect to God or are they one in the same?*

I mean I been thinking about that because I know I turned my head in court and saw you say, you forgive me, but I'm having a hard time believing it because I can't forgive myself. Can you help me out here? Again, I miss you. I apologize, and I love you, Jay,

Dee.

Jason,

I know I just wrote you a letter the other day, but I wanted to write another one to wish you a happy birthday baby boy. I know I been here like six months, but I ain't forgot about some of what's happening on the outside. I got happy as shit this morning when I woke up because I forgot I was here. I kept thinking about what I was going to do for your birthday this year. Remember that one year I took you to 131 Main just outside of Charlotte when we were stationed out at Lejeune. And you ordered the swordfish. I thought I was introducing you to some swanky shit. But little did I know about the Jason Williams experience. We had so much fun that weekend. I miss being able to be a foodie with you.

I got happy as shit thinking about how we used to test the liberty rings on our birthdays. I also miss trying to upstage your nigga Harry in the gift department. Like that Tag Heuer you refused to wear because you respected the man you were with.

I was thinking about what I was going to do this year until I woke up this morning and heard the sounds of inmates and the ventilation of the Brig. My new home. I don't have a watch to give you or mode of transportation to take you to an expensive five-star restaurant this year. I don't have anything but memories on paper to give you this year, Jay. Maybe that's better than me trying to buy you some shit. Because your ass has lived all over the world since you were a kid. Grew up in and toured Europe. You got your license driving a Benz on the fucking Autobahn. And you are so nonchalant about all that. It's funny how our realities shape our personalities. I mean, I came from privilege and you were privileged and appreciated what life gave you while you had it. I get bored with shit the minute it's out of the box.

What could I have possibly done to impress you? What was it about me out of all of the shit you had going on, stop and notice my messed up in the head ass? Because it wasn't my wallet or my influence that got you. You never cared about that type of shit. And I respect that.

JAY

I remember you told me a story about how your mama would let you run off to the toy section and look at the toy cars. Your fascination with cars was an interesting thing to me. You had me dying telling me that you would get so excited from looking at the Matchbox cars and the detail that they had that you would have to go take a quick piss break from a nervous bladder. Ol' Motor City face ass! You remember telling me that? According to you, they were the most authentic looking toy cars? I was a Hot Wheels kid, though. You know I'm a flashy nigga. I'm from the Chi. Everythang gots ta be loud! Nigga, you know even my weed gots ta be louder than my dads Harley, you know me!

But yo', I remember you telling me that you saw the Matchbox version of the new Dodge Dakota that came out in '89. You begged your mama to get it but she kept saying no so your ass snuck it on the belt at the register anyway. When you got home, your mama beat your ass over that toy truck, but you got to keep it. Matchbox should cut you a check, Jay, because that's dedication to the brand. Ol' loyal I'm gonna risk an ass whooping for a toy face ass.

Man, Jason, you almost had me in tears this morning when I thought about you telling me that story. I still can't believe out of all the things you've owned; you miss that the most because of your carelessness with it by leaving it sitting on the kerosene heater in the living room causing the wheels to melt.

So today, that's what I got you for your birthday, Jay. In my mind unfortunately, but I know it would mean the world to you if I could have really gotten you that little red toy truck with the chrome wheels and roll bar you loved. It would be the start of the least I could do since I took so much from you. I love you, man. Happy Birthday, Jay!

Dee

MS. EM

I sauntered into the cozy room I was staying in after a late-night stroll with the dog and suddenly felt alone. Not lonely. Alone. Here I was retracing my steps in a now semi-familiar city, unaware that I was estranged from myself with reckless abandon. I stopped envying the closeness Gary and my friends have with their families a couple years ago. I started believing that that lifeline in my bloodline wouldn't regain a pulse. Gary had a pulse. Then he didn't. He lived. He walked to his own beat. Confident. I felt like an accessory, to his murder, sometimes. But where did that leave me? I saw the door to my birdcage open. I was my very own. I was free, I guess. *Is this what it's supposed to feel like? Maybe at first,* I thought.

For the first time I guess I wasn't in a rush to fix something. I wasn't in a hurry to get somewhere. I wasn't disinfecting my Operatory to get to my next billable patient. I wasn't in a hurry to spend the money I made. I wasn't in a hurry doing meal prep and laundry. I wasn't worried about the debt I need to hurry up and pay, so I can hurry up and retire with a 401K. Getting home only to rush through the house I rushed to buy after rushing out of a relationship. However, a brotha' still needs to eat.

I was finally able to sit my black ass down and breathe. I actually had time to chill, rebuild me, and plan my next move? I started putting together a business plan a while back as I mentally prepared to return to reality at some point. I figured I could open my own hygiene/preventive dental care office and contract clients from the local provider network within the city. This was an idea I discussed a year or so ago with a doctor I used to moonlight for. I stopped the sale of my house before I left Chicago. I decided to use the money I acquired to pay what I owed on it and go from there. Mike agreed to housesit on the weekends with some strict instructions while I'm away. Lord only knows what is going on though. The only thing I'd have left to do would be to put my business model into practice and I'd be my own boss. *YES! Something positive at last!*

My phone vibrated loudly in the background. I hadn't paid attention to it much since I've been here. I turned the light on, walked over to the nightstand and sat on the bed. I picked up the phone and tapped ACCEPT.

"Hey, Mama," I said casually lying back on the bed not really wanting to be bothered at the moment. I had to face her sooner or later though. I moved the phone away from my face. I closed my eyes and took a very deep breath and held it preparing for Janice Ann to cut up with her *I'm still your mama* spiel. I released my breath and placed the phone to my ear in the middle of her first paragraph...

"...and you can't pick up a phone to at least say you weren't in the massive car crash on the news on CNN.

Some 27 car pile up on the Dan Ryan from all the flooding from that big storm today, killing people, and where are you? Why ain't you called nobody? What are you doing?" she said as I turned the speaker feature on. I laid the phone on my chest.

"Mama," I said pausing, "which one, out of that barrage of questions would you like me to answer first?" I said trying hard not to make that smart comment sting as much as I wanted it too.

"Boyyyyyy, the one where you watch your damned mouth! I am not Jasmine! Or one of your little...*friends*," she scolded.

"I wasn't trying to be smart, mother," I lied. She hated when I called her mother. So that was my subtle way of letting her know I really was.

"Jason. Where are you at?" she demanded in a brisk snap. "I been calling your cell phone, that dentist you said you worked for, and I called your house and some strange country sounding man answered your line, ain't no..."

"Mama. I'm in Paris," I snapped back proudly. I knew that was not going to go over well with her. I braced myself against my own laughter covering my mouth as the ocean waves crashed.

"PARIS...! You in...Jason, how long have you been gone boy!? This boy is over in a daaaaamn FOREIGN country! And ain't told no *damn* body? I am going to kick your behind when I see you! You know you really need to grow up and stop doing these up and at'em plans of yours?! Maybe something will click in that head of yours this year for your birthday. What about your job? You can just take vacation like that? Living that sinful lifestyle chasing after something you ain't got NO business chasing after...!" I just let her rant. I was over her negativity which I had endured for yeeeeears! I sat the phone on the bed and went to the terrace to push the doors open further. She was still going at it. I casually walked back over to the bed smiling, laid back down, put the phone back on my bare chest, closed my eyes, and PAID IT!

"Hello! Jason!?"

"I'm here, mother."

"Boy! Well answer me then, dammit!" she said. I chuckled wondering why I let this nonsense irritate me for so long.

"Okay. Let's see. Umm, I've been gone about five months. What else...ummm...I sifted my boyfriend's last remains, excuse me, his ashes..."

"Jason," she said warning me, but I kept going.

"...through my fingers, at the request of his mama, and because I loved him in spite of our mistakes..."

"Jason, that's enough," she warned a second time. I ignored her. She was going to hear what I had to say tonight, goddamn.

"And ooooo! The cherry on the sundae, Mama! I'm reading his killer's letter's to make sense of *what*? I don't know. Because I feel mad guilty, sometimes. Let's see, oh yeah, I helped to celebrate his parents beautiful 45th wedding anniversary because she actually gets along with her husband enough to stay in marital bliss. I mingled with his amazing family onboard this luxurious yacht circling this beautiful tropical island paradise. But I couldn't really enjoy the air, Ma! You know why? Because I listened to the police detective assigned to the murder case, who told me to use Vapo Rub under my nose to drive out the smell of Gary's blood. NOTHING smells or tastes like it use too! So Ma, this *lifestyle* that you scoff at, is my life! And I say this with as much respect as I can possibly give you right now, but you ain't even got your life squared away! PLEASE leave me alone about who needs to grow up, because Lord knows you might need a parrot to repeat that statement *ANYTIME* you enter a room," I said finally taking a breath feeling like I had conquered Mt. Kilimanjaro. I figured she was going to do one of two things, hang up or *GO IN!* It felt good to read Janice Ann to filth. This was another tick mark on my bucket list. YES!

"You listen to me, you may think you have life figured all the way out, but you are never too old to listen to sound advice from time to time. I'm your mother and you only get one..." she said before I interrupted her next tirade with,

"You seem to forget that you only *have* one son, Mama! Last I checked! Unless you're on a waiting list for a new uterus!" I snapped. There was a long pause. I could hear her angry breathing on the other end. So I knew she hadn't hung up.

"I'm going to let that slide this time because you have been through...a lot...I must say. Listen...you let that be your last time letting months go by and not checking in with your damn mama, little boy! You hear me?" I gagged because I was just waiting for her to be knocking down that good gay door.

"Yes," I said holding my ground. I only needed a pennant flag.

"What are you doing? Are you alright? And don't give me no more of them smart answers, either, L. J." she said.

"I'm fine," I said.

"How did Audrey treat you?" she asked of Gary's mother with an undertone of jealousy in her voice. I smiled.

"She was nice enough," I stated.

"You all right?"

"I'm trying to find out, Ma," I said rolling my eyes.

"Hmmm, you're back to being vague," she mused.

"Speaking of vague? What's up with you and my daddy?" I asked. I hadn't heard either of them talking about the subject of staying married in the last few months.

"Well, you know me and B.J. decided to go through with the divorce," she said somberly. I sucked my teeth.

"Hmmm. You're back to being a Mosley."

"Look, we just lost what we had in each other. It didn't feel safe anymore. Plus, I kissed some other man and I...I liked it," she said giggling like a schoolgirl.

"Ma! Really?" I asked trying not to picture her kissing some random dude.

"Boy, hush! So you can kiss a man, but I can't?" She said laughing. I gagged. Batman jumped up on the bed and started licking me. I moved him away from my face and he jumped up on my chest licking the phone.

"Batman, will you move," I laughed grabbing the phone wiping his spit off of the screen. "Touché. I guess you can now, Mama. I don't want to take your man kissing privileges away."

"Well, imagine how I feel, Jason, with all that happened and with what you're doing now..."

"Two separate scenarios, Mama."

"I guess this is really you, huh? You won't budge. As hard a time as it is to think of my son that way." She paused, took a breath, and finished her thought. "I'm just not a coddling type of woman, okay? But I'm still your mother," she said.

"Yup," I said rolling my eyes. I started petting Batman who had laid his head on my stomach.

"I don't have to agree with your decisions and you don't have to agree with mine. I am your mama, and you are my child. But you're a grown man. We all have to answer to God for our own, well, let's just forgive and move forward, okay?" she said.

"After you," I answered plainly.

"What does that mean?"

"Ma?"

"What?"

"I know the whole story about how you had me young and blah, blah, blah. But what was your dream? Didn't you have a dream you wanted to accomplish? Something you wanted the world to have? Something that you thought defined the very core of who you are...or were?"

"Jason, my dream was to make sure I took care of me and my two kids and that I introduced them to Jesus. Black woman defined. Mission accomplished," she said as I sucked my teeth.

"Ma, that's a duty not a dream. I mean, didn't you have something that just called out to you?" I asked trying to get her to think outside of her little box.

"Boy, what are you talking about?" she asked laughing.

"Never mind," I replied sharply not giving a damn about it anymore.

"How about I get back to you on that, Jason?"

"Mm hm."

"You be safe with them people out there. And since you gon' be *that way*, don't be over there *messing* with none of them ol' funky white boys. You hear me?" Mama said being nobody *BUT* Janice Ann.

"I can't," I chuckled, recalling my little white lie. "Ma, how about you be *safe*. I'm not the one who needs the strange man speech," I said shaking my head.

"I'm grown!" she huffed.

"And so am I, per your quote," I smiled.

"Bye, boy." She said laughing.

"Au revoir!" I said dismissing her with a loud shady French goodbye.

The clock read 11:33PM. I walked out onto the terrace to admire the nighttime view. Batman trotted behind me. I felt lighter now that I faced some things I needed to let go. It was nice to be away, but a part of me wondered what was floating in the crews Kool-Aid. For some strange reason hearing a raunchy story about some boy Michael treated as a sex toy on one of his "extended" lunch breaks would be cool to roll my eyes at right about now. Now that Janice Ann was checked off my to-do list as, read, the only thing left to process was what I've been reading...

L-WORD

Man, I ain't gon' say I'm scared of this right here, shawty, but I'm scared. Because I ain't never got jealous over no boy in nobody club. But Corey pissed me off staying out a little past the time we discussed he'd be hanging with his friends. Talm' bout he lost track of time after he ran into his ex, who wanted to *talk*. He claim ain't shit happen. I blurted out some shit in front of his friends about why he'd be stupid enough to visit a house that's already burnt down. Just flexin my nuts off that drank. He ain't like what I said an' I won't tryin' to hear nothin' he was scramblin' to explain. I need my lil' bro Jason to talk me off this ledge, cause I'm ready to jump ship. But something got me holdin' on to this man. I ain't never felt this before. I think I actually believe him.

I mean how da hell I go from eatin' more ass in a day than real food to blue balls waitin' to see where this shit gon' go? This some ol' faggoty bullshit right here! I need some ass bad and I'm trying not to power up my "hoe to go" phone, to bust down one of my gold member's. Some top-notch hood neck would feel nice right now. That's what I liked about my IHOP piece on Friday nights after the Prop. I'd get a short stack with a side of thoatk! Damn, Corey got me on this love bullshit.

I put my phone in my pocket and got up to walk upstairs to look through one of my bags. I opened it and reached in to take a look at temptation. My mind was telling me shit, go for it bruh, but my heart was like, man chill out dawg. I closed the bag and sat in the dark for a second looking out the window listening to the storm outside. I'm a country boy, so when it's storming outside all I want to do is turn the lights out and make "it" disappear. I unzipped the bag and snatched the phone out and walked back down to the living room. I opened the patio door and put the screen in place. I looked out at the light show leaning up against the beam. One hand wrapped around the hoe-to-go phone, and the other in my sweatpants with a semi-hard dick.

The mist from the downpour hit my arm. One of my bust downs used to watch me fuck his nigga on the balcony of they condo downtown. I used to slow stroke that shit killing that second hole with the lightening flashing over the 27th floor. The harder it rained, the harder I beat that shit, watchin' them phatt ass cheeks dribble against my thighs. My mind was on swell weighing the consequences with the water splashing outside. I thought about how wet that shit be as I sat the phone on the coffee table. I pulled off my wife beater and put my headphones on. I raised the volume up on the stereo and took some frustration out with my weights on the living room floor. Twenty minutes in, I saw the phone glowing letting me know I had a call. I stopped what I was doing and smiled catching my breath once I saw the name...

"Who dick, you suckin'?" I said waiting for an answer.

"Ooooo, yours tonight, Big daddy! Especially with that ol' sexy raspy voice you got, telling me what to do," the caller replied.

"Oh, we can get that crackin' right now, lil' daddy. You been missin' dis fat nine of mine, ain't you?" I said smiling.

"Mmm hmm. I stay missin' that dick."

"I miss eatin' dat phat ass,"

"Do you?"

"Fuckin' right. So, you gon' lem'me, buss up that vagina tonight? Pull 'em lips back and shit?" I asked leaning back against the sofa, sliding my hand in my pants.

"Okay, hag! See, I can't do this. Vagina lips, though?!" Jason said bursting into laughter.

"You know I'm about that boogina," I laughed.

"Yeah, it goes down on the DM's! What the hell are you up too, slut bag?" Jason replied.

"I'm maintaining, bae bro, how you?"

"I'm getting there, Mike. It's been rough, but I'm cool. You alright?"

"Hornier than a bitch, but I'm good. Why's it been rough, what's going on?" I said looking out the window. Finally able to take a moment from thinking about my dumb shit.

"Mikie." He paused and sighed. "I'm sorry I've been in and out, but man..." He stopped.

"What happened Jason?" I asked.

"Dude, this shit was the hardest, Mike...I thought I was done thinking about what happened." I could hear that he was sniffling.

"It's okay Jason. I'm here bae bro," I smiled. He was finally about to talk to me about what he was feeling, I thought.

"The day we let his ashes go, I swear to you, I could feel him swirling around me...and it was like his hand was letting go of mine. Mike, I had this weird peace about his death. This peace about all this, I mean it's done, right?" He said. I could still hear sniffling, followed by him blowing his nose. I had never seen Jason cry in person, and hearin' him crying was breaking my heart.

"Jason, I wish I was there with you."

"I do too, but hey, I'm good." He sniffled and laughed. "*Wheeew!* Okay, I'm back,*"*

"So does that mean you made peace with *everythang*?" I asked.

"If you're talking about Darius, that's the part I think has me trippin'."

"You read any of them letters?" I asked.

"Yeah. I initially decided to randomly pick four letters to read..."

"Why four?" I interrupted.

"I asked Siri," he said.

"For real?" I laughed.

"Yes,"

"So you not gon' read the rest?"

"Yes. I've been slowly reading them in my travels, and,"

"Wait! Where you at, now?"

"In my draws island hopping, so, like I was saying," he started while I interrupted his next line. I was trying to make sense of everything, then I remembered this is Jason I was talking to.

"How much money did this nigga lea' you, shawty? Damn!" I asked curious as shit.

"Enough. He was extravagant in many things, but spending wasn't one of them. But this is my money I'm spending, though. Lucky for me I listened to the CDR I worked for when I was stationed in Lejeune who put me on to a few investments he helped me start. They finally matured, and blah, blah, blah. Like it or not, we deal in emotions, and they deal in economics." Jason said casually.

"Damn, you ain't tell me you was balling out of control, shawty, shit! His parents ain't try to fight you over it?"

"Michael!"

"What?"

"I picked *FOUR RANDOM* letters," he paused and laughed. "And this dude, Darius man! You think you know somebody, but if you only knew the behind the scenes footage. Man it's a good thing we don't know everything that God knows."

"What was this nigga talkin' about?" I asked.

"Well," I heard him let out a breath. "He killed. Okay, to me it sounded like he was...well in one of the letters it sounded like he planned to and had every intent and motive, in his mind to kill Gary, maybe even me. He had both of us in his sights for different reasons."

"Are you fucking serious, Jason? Daaamn!" I said laying all the way down on the couch.

"Yeah, man, what I read creeped me the hell out."

"Are you all right, though? About what happened and all?" I asked throwing my leg over the backrest.

"I wish I knew. I'm want to make sure I understand what he wrote. I'm still wrapping my brain around how he illustrates that th..." He stopped talking and took a breath. "Yo', we'll talk about it when I get back."

"Yeah, when you're ready. It's cool. Jason, man, I'm sorry about all this. What can I do to help bae bro?" I asked hoping there was an answer. I know what its like to lose someone with little understanding of it.

"I don't know, Mike."

"When you coming back to the Chi?"

"Lo'Key! What am I coming back too?" He said.

"You still got a home here."

"Yeah." He sighed. "I do."

"So you gon' read some more?"

"I think I'm done for a minute. I'm not even done with July's stack." He chuckled.

"What you gon' do with them?"

"It will come to me. I may burn that junk. Love will make people do some bullshit, Mike." He said. There was a silent pause that I broke...

"So how is your momma?"

"Chile, Janice Ann is still up to her old ego trips. She ain't gon' change. I let her HAVE IT though, Mike! She wasn't ready!" he laughed.

"Y'all always letting each other have it."

"I know right! We need to cut that crap out."

"Her and your dad alright?"

"Man, hell naw! She ran him off just like her sisters, Patti and Selma, ran off they husbands," he chuckled. "I been talking to my dad off and on, and his notes look similar to mine, minus the gay shit."

"What you mean?" I laughed.

"It means that we're getting too old for her bullying." Jason said, "What's going on with you these days?"

"Ain't shit. I been studying for the test," I lied right fast.

"A pregnancy test?" He said being funny.

"The Navy exam fool," I laughed.

"Hmm, so your, by the book LPO let you take the late exam. You been real shady surrounding your body count."

"I have been, bae bro', the fuck! I gotta make rank." I said laughing.

"Okay. I'm just saying. As long as you ain't turning my house into a brothel," he laughed. "Turnstile! We have another division! Your name better be on that advancement list." He said laughing, shouting an old Navy boot camp phrase, depicting men lining up at the galley door for meal service.

"Watch, and you just be glad you ain't sale it. Wishy washy ass. Your house is fine. And so is your lawn guy with them thick ass thighs."

"Yeah, Wayne is a cutie. He's about as straight as 9:45, though."

"Yeah, I noticed," I laughed. "Where you going to next cause you ain't gon' be no good coming back here to this cold," I asked.

"I'm still trying to figure out my life. I've been putting a plan together I think might work for me in terms of income."

"Fuckin' right! Do tell?" I said glad to hear he was getting his mind right.

"I'm going to open my own hygiene practice. With two spaces I'll charge rent for and lease to independent contractors. It ain't quite ready yet, but I feel good about it. So don't go telling everybody."

"Jason! That sound like a good plan to me. Being your own boss and shit. I loves it." I said.

"I know right. So, I'll be home for my birthday, queen. Again, I want to stay under the radar, Mike! Don't go running your mouth."

"Jason, who I'ma tell?" I said smiling from ear to ear. Wait, that's still a long ass time away, like months away."

"January is right around the corner, boy."

"What are you going to do for Christmas? Jason, come on man. You killin' me."

"I haven't thought about Christmas."

"Well I can't wait to see you," I said still excited as fuck.

"I'll email you my itinerary. Cool?" Jason said.

"Yeah, that's cool. Can you at least try to be here fo' the New Years?"

"I'm terminating this conversation," he chuckled.

"I just miss you being around. I love you. That's all."

"I miss you too, top! Now man up. I gotta go."

"A'ight bae bro'! Be safe out there and suck a lil' of dat island dick or sum'n. I know you need to fuck." I laughed.

"Perhaps," he laughed. "I'll talk with you later. And keep your doggone mouth closed. And don't be hoeing in my house. It's bad enough you got a Cadillac on blades parked in my driveway," Jason warned.

"A'ight! Bye boy," I laughed immediately brainstorming and channeling my pinned-up energy into planning the crunkest birthday/welcome back party Jason has ever seen! That's also the same time as Battle of the Bands. So this gon' be crunk! He deserves a pick me up. I'll deal with Corey later on. My bae bro was gettin' ready to come home! Turn up!

PEN

So damn. It was time to get back to reality and go home. Batman and I woke up to a rainy January morning, yet, the sun was shining. Sun showers always fascinated me. Something good always comes after one. It wasn't gloomy and the shimmering flecks of rain played peek-a-boo with the quilted clouds in the sky's pink backdrop. I gave the Creator thanks in silent prayer for giving me one last gorgeous view in bed through the window of the brightly colored postmodern building. I stroked Batman's head and neck, listening to the sound of raindrops compete with his pants.

It was time to go home. It meant something different this time. I had this feeling before, but this had assurance. I had built the confidence to rebuild myself and reclaim Jason. Life seemed to be onboard with me, because the unexpected curve ball that hit me hard in the stomach before, swung around a little higher this go round. The heart.

My dad called me this morning. We had a candid talk of how he felt about his marriage going the direction it did. He apologized for the way he let mama influence his feelings toward me. We talked about my situation as he helped me to logically understand the issues going on in my world. The questions he had and the personal stuff we discussed were things I daydreamed talking to my dad about. The answers amazingly showed how much of a parallel our lives were.

Two grown ass men crying. Two grown ass men reintroducing themselves to one another. Two grown ass men giving the other permission to speak freely. No issue, stereotype, or misconception off limits. Two men of the same blood coming together in Spirit and our own individual truths as a father and a son. He explained to me that sometimes desire does more than ignite into flames. Sometimes it gets too hot to contain and brings the structure down to its foundation. He also said...

"L. J., life is going to chase you some of everywhere. You are going to want to run away from the man you know you were called to be. But you'll reach a point where you stop, stand still, and patiently start to live your own life. Be that man. A progressive man I raised you to be. Not every man will have the answers, but every man will find *his* answers. Be the best at whatever you know you're s'pose to be."

"Yes, sir," I said as his words rang in my head with this God-like tone.

"Hear me good. You're my son and I love you. In spite of, okay," he said not holding back his thoughts.

He began to pray for me. Not at me. With me this time, thoroughly changing the dynamic of our relationship and what it could be now. I was glad because I didn't need to talk to my dad about gay shit. I needed my dad's advice on life. I was about to make some moves and I needed his wisdom and life experience. It felt good to know we could start from there. Elements so commonplace in our society yet taken for granted.

It was a few days before my 28th birthday. I walked out onto the balcony one last time before taking a taxi to the airport. I took in the beautiful views of Puerto Rico, the last spot on my island tour. I was going to miss waking up on a beach and doing the absolute least, but I feel like I got so much more done than I have in years passed. This trip was healing me in ways I didn't see coming. Many things and ideals didn't fit anymore. God looked even bigger than I was taught or even shown. I think I was prepared for what was next.

The cabbie pulled in front of Terminal B and carried Batman's cage and my bag to the curb. I tipped him and made my way to the ticket counter to check my luggage and the watch dog. The line in security wasn't that bad, I thought, as I turned the music down, I had blasting from my ear buds. I took off my shoes and emptied my pockets. I was in my own world standing behind this very handsome brotha who had a mature but boyish look and a nicely trimmed full beard. Maybe I was standing to close. He bumped into my shoulder hard trying to take his bag off.

PEN

"My bad, bruh. I didn't mean to hit you," he said with a look of concern on his face.

"It's cool, man. I'm built Detroit tough," I laughed.

"Oh, you from the D?" he asked as we inched forward placing our things in our respective bins.

"Yes, I am," I said not really trying to hold a conversation or flirt.

"I was born there too, bruh," he said.

"That's cool," I stated wishing I had my music or maybe a different place in line. *Please hurry up TSA people*, I thought.

"I got family out that way," he smiled. "We could be related, or somethin'," he said just before he moved through the metal detector and waited for his bin.

I stepped through as he grabbed his items and walked over to a seat to put his stuff back on. The agent waved her magic wand over my body before I retrieved my bin. I sat down and put my shoes on before stuffing my headphones into my ears. I had forgotten about ol' boy just that quickly until he walked up to me extending his hand just as I was about to stand up. That's when I noticed he had me by a couple inches. But at my height, that doesn't take much. My favorite hip-hop track by The Roots was playing. It was right at the height of *MY PART*, so I was slightly irritated when I had to press pause. It probably showed on my face.

PEN

"You can call me Pen. You look sooo familiar, man," he offered with bright pearly whites and his calloused hand still out. I reluctantly shook it thinking, *Clown, NOOOOO!! We is not about to bust down in one of these bathroom stalls, right quick! Beat it!* I grabbed the now empty bin pasting one of those fake white people smiles on my face. You know the one they make when they're scared to return a hello to some strange colored man.

"Pen...? That's cute," I said, giving him a sexy smize with dimples. I brushed past him noticing how good he smelled, restarting my favorite jam in my ear buds. He was smiling and staring at me as we went our separate ways. I walked into a shop to get some water.

When I headed to my gate, I noticed he was nursing a Guinness at one of the sports bars nearby. The only TV showing auto sports had his undivided attention. I found that interesting but tried to think nothing further of it. I took a few more glances at him from where I could see him trying to figure out if his face looked familiar to me. A flashback of déjà vu sent a shiver down the small of my back when a vivid close view of his eyes came to mind. Eyes so innocently bright, searching for something good to reflect. There was something vaguely familiar about them, but I couldn't say why.

He wasn't anyone I would say is family. But with both my grandfather's respective track records, you never know. He was *very* handsome, and I was trying to stop looking at him and focus on the car magazine I had probably wasted more than seven dollars on. His thick fingers pawed the bottle, bringing frosty swigs of beer to his luscious lips, peeking through that sexy beard.

I drank some of my water and got caught up in the music blaring in my ears again. Several planes were lining the jet way ready to take off. A slight scan of the room had me abruptly turn my head just as "Pen" stood up and hoisted that big ass duffle bag over his broad shoulders. I chuckled when he secured the straps to his body. He adjusted his blue fitted cap and carried his cute teddy bear frame towards the opposite end of the terminal. I felt that urge to put feelings to paper that I'd been ignoring lately. The desire was lacking, but the need was there. My eyes followed him until he disappeared into the rush of the crowd. The few words Pen told me, the kindness he tried to show me lingered. The word 'familiar' reminded me that I hadn't gripped a pen since I wrote Gee my best last goodbye. That's what I was calling him now. For some reason it's just what he became.

All of this shit ended over a letter. He was mad at all the letters written from a secret love I adored. Letters forming words of what that love and I could be if I just gave him more time. He found left over emotions and feelings that didn't belong to him on slips of paper I never had the courage to mail. Just one letter in particular that I wrote to Darius showing how I really felt about him. A possible once upon a time no longer tucked away. One letter written during the break-up heard round the Chi. One letter that I decided wouldn't be a good idea to send. Words I put together with care and patience ensuring that I got it all out. How maybe I thought Dee-Jay could have been something dope. The night of his death, we were arguing over a response written with my favorite pen.

Gee gave it to me. There was this poem that I had started before I went to visit him in Chicago the first time. I recited the first part to him and he was like, *Yo, babes! You have to finish that before you leave*. He gave me this thick green wooden pen he had lying around. I nicknamed it the pickle and of course his mannish tail took the opportunity to joke about it being thick like his dick. That doggone thing became my go-to writing tool when I got lost in the alphabet. I remember finishing that poem, yet I cannot recall what I did with it. It was the first piece I wrote for him and it wasn't even about him.

That letter was the first piece I wrote about love that wasn't about Gary. I was writing to find answers. Maybe hopeful closure to what was gray in either situation. I wrote Darius free verse start to finish, no editing. I felt like I could have written so much more, but the pickle ran out of ink somewhere before the last period. I remember feeling the need but no desire to continue an unfinished flow I never re-read. Sometimes, I wonder if any of those missing words would have spared a life. A pen is the only

PEN

personification I know that has an excuse to run out of words to finish a love story...

UPENDO REIGN

Mom gave me a name that writes its own story. Upendo. Mom found it in a book of African names she had. Yoo-Pen-Doo. She said I was a love child of sorts. Close, but not like the tragedy Diana Ross sings about. She was a young fly girl turned future single mother her junior year of high school. My dad as she tells it, had dreams of moving to California and being an architect. He wanted to be the next Paul Williams, studying his craft and designing houses for celebrities like he did. I don't know if he succeeded or not. But Mom said he definitely had the talent and skill to possibly do so.

The two of 'em knew each other from around the way, becoming high school sweethearts freshmen year at the famous Cass Technical High School in Midtown Detroit when it was the shit. Mom said she fell hard for him. He was tall, dark, thin, and fine. Spoiled rich kid. She thought he felt the same way until he said she was trying to trap him with a damn kid as if she was the only one in bed doing the nasty. When she told him she was pregnant, things changed. Immediately. He looked at her like she was on sale. And all of a sudden, he transferred, and she lost touch with him.

Everyone told her she needed to get rid of "it." She didn't need that kind of burden. Her dad, my grandfather, was a single father of four. Three boys, plus her, plus me in his eyes made five look like a tie with the Saint Bernard roaming the backyard. He felt since she was grown and willing to spread her legs at 16, she was grown enough to spread her wings out of his nest. "Go make that boy man up!" Her heart had been broken twice because she was his pride and joy. Once daddy's little girl, the apple of his eye, my mom never looked at men quite the same. And she wouldn't even say anything to Gramps. She doesn't trust men. Maybe she didn't understand us. I do my best to remain the exception.

She said she started showing early, and the only one on her side was Great Gram who unfortunately lived in Chicago. So she finished that last semester of school, packed up, and left all she knew and moved to the Chi a month after I was born. Her motivation was Great Gram telling her, "Be and give the world what you want it to have, child. You can't fret about what others give the good Lord back in return." When she came across my name, and she spoke it out loud, it exited me in the womb tickling her senses. She said it was a different kind of kick I did. She felt something soothing in it. So Love is what she named me. And love is what she gave me. I became her world.

Mom put everything she had into me. She put her life on hold to take care of me. She eventually finished college because she had Great Gram's support. We stayed with her up until it was time for me to leave the nest. Great

Gram lived to be 102 years old and that old lady was still strong and in her right mind up until the day she died. She had so many stories and had done so much with her time here. She left her house to Mom, who passed it to me. That Duplex was a hub in the neighborhood. People would stop by to check on us and make sure we had what we needed when things were a little rough. She helped organize the block parties every summer to help the neighborhood kids get school supplies and lunch ticket money for the year. I used to hang the banner she quilted. No child should ever go without LOVE. Mom and Great Gram and the community we lived in looked out for one another in ways that barely happens these days. I wasn't a part of a system, rather a kinship. That black awareness in fellowship. Unity.

I write my own story, which is why I go by, Pen. It makes it easier anyway. People are always jacking up my name. So, I simply tell'em, You can call me, Pen. And I smile with it, cause it helps. Especially since a I'm a muscled dark-skinned man. I took the poor man's route into school by joining the Navy. I didn't want Mom to stress over no more bills. I had a thing for building shit as a kid. Loved a good ol' Lincoln Log set. I decided to be a part of the Navy Construction Force, NCF, better known as the SeaBee's. I learned all I thought I needed to know from carpentry, flooring, laying foundation, electrical work, and using heavy duty commercial equipment. I certified and qualified in everything I could get my hands on. My endgame was erecting my own buildings and houses, to make money with my two bare hands. I wanted to rebuild Great Gram's house. Maybe have my own crew. I wanted to help my black people not have to rely on no white man. I paid my dues. I signed 10 years of life away. I had to take a risk and start somewhere.

Sometimes I think that my dad's blood was pulling me towards him. To maybe find out what happened to that nigga. Or to find out about the part of him in me Mom never knew. The parts of me that didn't make sense to her because he was the missing part in our lives. Who knows man. I ended up in California to train. I loved it out that way. Holly-weird ass shit! I easily see why he wanted to trade nine months of cold and snow for 365 days of sunshine. But I spent most of my tour in Okinawa, Japan. Probably one of the more interesting places a black kid from the hood could learn to love. I didn't mind the hard work of being a SeaBee and the crap I took at times. The stress. The bullshit. The camaraderie. The Hail and Farewells. And oh yeah. Me being queer. That shit sucked. But I had an endgame. I had a goal. I had a plan. I couldn't let my dick get in the way like my dad's. And I couldn't end up unhappy never trusting love like Mom.

I finally took a real week off from life to go to a beach resort in the Puerto Rico. That's all I did. Just chill. Only thing that was missing was a lil' cutie. It rained this morning, but it was sunny at the same time. I never seen no shit like that where I'm from. Not even in Oki. The rock. It would have been nice to do that with someone. I walked in the rain on the beach like the big kid cheesing, before check- out. It's only been a week. But for me that's a long break. A week to regroup. A week to sit down. Mom said I was burning myself out. She stopped me, "I'm doing this for your own good. You need to live sometime, baby." She bought my trip as a just because gift and said, "Go!" She knows I'm a workaholic and felt like maybe this would cause me to go out and meet some cute guy to bring home to meet her, and woo, woo, woo. Maybe I was scared of my own name and what the letters translate to in Swahili.

"Mom, you don't understand how this whole black queer thing works," I'd tell her. She'd tell me, "Y'all make this shit so complicated. Two men in they feelings trying not to be in 'em." It's about sex, not love. And these niggas want that dick that I used to be happy to give 'em, but the shits boring these days. I'm all about gettin' ass. I'm a Leo. I'm a Lion. I like to hunt, and niggas make it waaay too easy. All the time trying to front. Looking like more than they are. The thrill of the chase is not even a thrill that's present. Not like it used to be. At least to me. Cause see, I'm looking for one that's on his grind like me. Match that shit, and you got my attention.

I'm hopeful. I'm a good man. I ain't the cutest but work hard. I take care of mine own. I got a nice solid gym body. I stand 5'10." I ain't no skinny nigga. I'm easy on the eyes, clean, tatted, stay smellin' good, I'm my own boss, and I turned 30 this past summer. Dag! Sitting out on the beach to recharge was probably a good thing. Think I'm ready for someone special, like Mom been saying. It kind of feel like that's missing. She ain't steered me wrong yet. When it came to me and Mom, there is no comfort zone. It's all or nothing.

True story. First ten months into my tour in Oki, beating my dick to imaginary thoughts in the open bay barracks they had us in wasn't cutting it. My black ass had the bright idea to log on to the government computer while on duty and print off a few screen shots of some phatt back shots. I ain't think I was gon' get caught. You know they tell you not to do all kinds of shit, just to say it sometimes. Kind of like parents. But me being Pen, did my own thang. Fuck 'em. Who knew they actually monitored that shit.

Anyway, I'm clicking, printing, and thinkin' 'bout stickin'. I pulled up all kinds of dirty gay shit, man. Mind you, this is pre-Obama Don't Ask, Don't Tell repeal. A week or so goes by, and it's been SeaBee business as usual. I'm on a sight learning the D9 Military Bulldozer, right. And I get summoned to Master Chief's office. That's not a good thing. At all. They sent Dinkin's punk ass to tell me. I squared myself away. Got as much grime off my boots as possible. Get to headquarters trying to feel out the situation before I enter the room. No one knows or is telling me what's up.

Finally, I get called back. My LPO, my Chief, Master Chief, the CO's secretary, and the battalion Master at Arms is there standing by. All white faces. All with sourpuss looks on 'em. They questioned me about my night on duty. Who was there? Who I spoke with? Who entered? When and what I had for chow? Did I complete my rounds? Who exited? Shit, even who pooted, my nigga, gad'damn! They scoured the duty logs, eventually getting to the incriminating evidence of the questionable material found on the cyber records during my watch. Basically, they wanted me to out myself without them doing it.

I called Mom collect after a three-hour interrogation. She and I talked and that was the first time I told her I liked men. She got me to chill. She didn't skip a beat, telling me to fess up to what I had done, and continue to be the good man she raised me to be. One of integrity that takes responsibility for his actions. Her words, If I don't give a damn who you stick your dangalang in, then damn it they shouldn't either, baby. Be your damn self, and I mean that. If they kick you out, you tell them yo' Mom got yo' back.

So you know they sent my black ass to Captain's Mast. That's an in-house trial to punish you. I gave not one fuck. I pressed the shit out of my cracker jack, and stood there in front of the whole command, squared away as always. Yeah, they made an example out of me. I was at Parade Rest listening to these crackas talk about what a good motivated Sailor I was, how this was a mistake, and that I didn't use the right judgment call. I was called a liar and I think, a pervert too. They even tried to say I corrupted the network with a virus. I was given no sympathy and had my feet held to the flames as they flashed the nude photos of Tiger Tyson, T. Malone, and a bunch of other big booty niggas I clicked on. They put all that shit on display trying to get a rise out of me. I didn't know whether to laugh my ass off or let my dick gon' and bust through my uniform when they got to a pic of a sexy cutie playing with his puckered star. Real shit. Was one of my favorites of the night.

Now once the humiliation ceased, the Skipper gon' ask if I had anything to say for myself. I figured I was on the first thing smoking, so fuck it. I popped tall and was like, "Sir, with all due respect, who I stick my dick inside shouldn't degrade the valuable asset I am to this battalion and the World's Finest Navy. Especially with all the money spent to train me. But you gon' do what you gon' do. This charade of pictures made that quite clear. I ain't been able to get my kind of sex, I was horny, and this was a quick fix to keep my head in the game. My bad. If you kick me out. Cool. If you keep me in. Cool. Either way I got this." He didn't know what to do with that statement but chuckle his ass off then said, "Reign, I like you. You've got balls! 45 days restriction. No outside liberty. And you better have enough pictures to last you until you PCS off this rock. Or get a damn laptop! Dismissed!" Me and the CO was cool as fuck after that. And that's my coming out story.

I called Mom to tell her it was all good. She was proud, if not embarrassed for me when I told her what they did. My unit didn't treat me any different. It was a big deal until it wasn't a big deal. They say a woman can't teach a man how to be a man, well, I disagree. I tell'em look at me. I've had to tell that story a couple times to get my point across. Because the most important things you can do as a man is to honor and take care of self and home. Have the courage to give back to God's people, your people. And manage your responsibilities and commitments in life no matter how small. That's how you earn respect. By being a man of integrity. So I look for that in the men I like. Even in a drought. I'm a man with an endgame. A plan.

This trip to the beach was one of Mom's better ideas. She could come up with some whoppers, man. But this was what I needed. *I needed this week,* I thought as I walked to the airport security. I felt good as shit and the beach had my skin feeling and looking right. I packed one duffle bag I didn't have to check. I hate all 'em extra fees and the bullshit they make you go through. So I pack light as I can. I started to loosen up the straps to take it off, but it slipped and hit this phyne lil' guy standing behind me. I could tell I had irritated him. He was so cute I had to at least try to get him to smile, since I almost broke his arm...

"My bad, bruh. I didn't mean to hit you," I said hoping he wasn't pissed off. He kind of rolled his eyes and took a deep breath.

"It's cool, man. I'm built Detroit tough," he giggled, which made me feel a little comfortable to say more. His lil' short ass was sexy as fuck. He had these dope ass chinky brown eyes that fucking glowed when he made eye contact with me. I wanted to know more. I was trying not to be too forward, but the Lion in me was up.

"Oh, you from the D?" I asked. I took a minute to stuff my shit into one bin.

"Yes. I am." His answer was dry but still friendly.

"I was born there too, bruh," I smiled checking to see if that was my in.

"That's cool," he said as dry as before. He slid his bin forward barely touching mine. I wanted to see that smile and them eyes again.

"I got family out that way," I said smiling at him. "We could be related, or somethin'," I said. He distracted me which caused the TSA lady to yell at me to take my turn through the metal detector.

I rushed through smiled and grabbed my stuff off the belt. I noticed they had paused the line, so I walked over to a seat to put my stuff on right quick. I looked up and saw lil' daddy hemmed up by the agent. I'm irritated, but I'm trying to be nice look he had on his face was so fuckin' cute. I was trippin' because a thought of what our first argument might look like came to mind. His jeans looked like they cost a little money judging by the way they fit his lean body. He sat down and put on these crisp graffiti style leather Chucks.

True story. It was something about this dude that felt familiar. I knew him from somewhere. I based this off of that smile and them eyes. But where? I don't forget a face, especially one as cute as his. Something told me to shoot another shot. He tossed his EarPods in, right as I walked up to him. I put my hand out to grip his. Lil' daddy stood up. That's when I noticed his height was perfect for me. He'd fit nice and snug up against Daddy. I bit my lip and smiled when I saw the irritation on his face again. That look he gave the TSA. He hit pause. When I knew I had his attention, I spoke.

"You can call me Pen. You look sooo familiar man," I was geekin' and shit staring in them eyes. Them shits excited me. Fuck! I could tell he didn't want to shake my hand. He picked up his bin and almost convinced me he was smiling for real.

"Pen...? That's cute," He sized my black ass up and brushed past me. I got a glimpse of the phatty he was sportin' behind that sag, though. He hit play again. I thought about following that ass to the store he walked too, but I felt like at that point I'd be playin' myself. He was phyne as fuck though. He probably thought I wasn't his type.

All of a sudden, I can't get this dude off my mind. He offered a challenge that woke something up in me. But damn. I didn't even know his name. But I had to get the green light. Was he going to Detroit? Was I going to have to take a flight to the D? Visit Gramps old cranky ass who I ain't seen in years? Put out a APB? I was trippin'. I know I was, because I thought about walking up and down the terminal to see if he might be going to Chicago. I was nursing a Guinness watching Auto Racing on one of the TVs. I did walk the terminal just to pass a little time. Not to look for him though. By the time I got to my gate they were boarding.

I jumped in line ready to get back to my city and my work. I bought the souvenirs everyone requested. Liquor. I got Mom some stuff too. I was looking forward to gettin' up with my niggas I grew up with. We were scheduled to hang once I got back in town. First up is Dave. If no other nigga know me, he do. His dad used to step in where mine was lacking, so I always had a father figure in my life even if Mom wasn't interested in entertaining a boyfriend. Our moms were close, so naturally, we became close.

Dave was the brain of the hood. He stood out like a sore thumb. He was always the tallest in a crowd, now standing 6'6". Solid 250. He's a chocolate brown teddy bear type with a baldie. Malcolm X glasses. Mandatory short cut beard. The sexy nerd is what the girls called him. Plus, he could sing his ass off in church or the cafeteria. He looked like he should be playing ball somewhere, but his head was into numbers like his dad. He's a CPA and tax consultant. He's my friend but more so my brother. I let him rent out the unit above me. He's also straight. Got some chick on his arm gassing him up these last six months. She ain't told him where she work. But that shit, my nigga, requires a whole other train of thought. My second day one, is Maseo. Now that's my bi-sexual homeboy. We used to kick it from time to time when we was young knuckleheads.

True story. Me and this nigga up in his room playing the Sega. I brought over the new Mortal Kombat Mom got for me. I was beating that ass until he finally won a round. He got all excited and we took a snack break then we started up again. Somewhere in the middle of a round, he started feeling on my leg. I didn't stop him. We kept looking forward until both of our characters were just swaying ready to, FIGHT! Controllers in hand. It felt like my dick was in his. Ready to fight, that is. We were 13. He gon' come with the, "My bad bro', I keep thinking you my girl." I'm like, "Nigga, yeah right! You know who I am." And that's how that started. We kept that up until school started again. I never looked at, Sega! quite the same. Nigga, got some knowledge on him. I ain't no easy shaft to handle. I call it the summer suck off of '93 we never speak of.

He seems to like women more in my opinion, but he always lets whoever he builds with know what's up. Let his ass tell it. Maseo is sexy as fuck. That's my bro' but he's a head turner. Light skinned, slim cut build, short tapered beard these days, deep waves, a real decent guy, but he always got some shit up his sleeve to blind side a motherfucka. That's what we call him, Mase. He sound like he country, but he Chi-town all day. South burbs where he lay. Because of his looks, he gets misjudged a lot of times, but it's more to Maseo than he's phyne. He makes a shit load of commission at the dealership he works at. I'm sure his looks are a motivating factor. No one wants to say no to a beautiful face. But the boy works hard and plays even harder.

To my surprise I stepped onboard the plane to see the mystery guy sitting in first class, lookin' right! He was reading the latest edition of Automobile Magazine. My suspicions? His gear, his plane ticket, that body, and his choice in auto reading material lead me to believe he's high maintenance. A conniving stunt? Won't know until I see how the inside of the crib look. That'll tell me what type of time I need to be on. Stuff it, or cuff it? *I'm thinking highly of you right now cutie,* I thought to myself. I sat my bag down and took my jacket off. Flexing through my t-shirt. The dope part is he lives in my kingdom. So, I know eventually I'll see him. With his phyne ass. Patience is my strong suit.

I was stuck behind this lady who took her sweet time putting her bags away. While I was stalled, I hoped he'd look up so we could lock eyes, but he was paying no one any attention sitting by the window. My perpetual pump flexed tribal ignored. He probably got a fucked-up crib. Some raggedy apartment out in the Wood. It always be the cute ones stunting in the airport. He probably stuck up as shit. For no reason. *Ay! Look at me, cutie!* I thought to myself. The woman in the aisle moved out of my way. Fuck. I shook my head, smiled, and walked to my seat. Maybe I'll stumble into him n'em Chi-town streets...

RETURN

One day I'm going to change sidewalks.

You never acknowledge my wave.

You just walk right by me like I ain't even there.

You don't acknowledge the care that I put into my stare,

And I'm guessing I scare you into more of the shell I see you creep into when my hand comes within view.

You walk right by me not acknowledging the nod that I bring.

You ignore my smile like being courteous is some petty thing.

You walk right the fuck by me like you don't even see me just inches away with a swift shoulder pass and not a single word to say.

You keep on walking,

And I just keep thinking that maybe one day you'll somehow see a deeper me.

One day you'll look up and observe something special about me.

And somehow become star struck.

You must have been hurt,

And that makes me wanna stop and ask,

What can I do to help chase away your blues?

But that might be just a bit too inventive for you.

RETURN

That's why I keep my cool,

Canceling another moment to look like a fool.

But how would you know when you just keep passing me by like some jerk?

You walk right the fuck by without giving me a reason why I shouldn't just walk another way.

I can't help myself.

It's you who I live and love to see day after day.

I'm probably foolishly taking time to pick out the right pair of jeans.

Doing my workouts with more than my health in mind,

Trying to ignore my hard peen.

I be lookin' so clean,

And you be lookin' so mean.

Maybe it's the right shoe,

Or some color that will pop your interest to finally spark a beginning.

But you'll have to run up the street to catch up to see,

Simply because you keep walking right by me.

And pardon my French, God,

But would it be too much to ask for a recalculated route away from this cute, sexy, mu'sucka right here?

This isn't fair.

I don't know if he's ignoring the possibility or if he's just unaware.

So my prayer for today is that he trips and falls into me with no excuse but to say,

Aww man,

I'm so sorry,

My bad.

By the way,

I planned those calculated missteps just to have a reason to ask what I practiced in one of my own imaginary scenes.

How was your day?

Outside of my crush linen daydreams I'll stay patient,

Fall back,

Remain discreet,

And keep walking up this block until either he or me decide to speak or stomp up a different street.

The bumpy motion of the jet woke me up out of the dream I think I was having about that strange guy in the airport. You can call me, Pen. Really, dude? He was...yeah, he had a cute thang happening. I just don't know if I'm ready to entertain no dude right now. Plus, he doesn't live in Chicago, so too bad so sad. I got too much I'm trying to do anyway when this plane lands. Its back to the grind.

A grind that's going to be on my terms. That's that beautiful part about it. I'm scared but it's a good kind of scared. I need to look at office spaces, I got to get my house back in order, Batman needs to go to the vet, I need to challenge the board to renew my hygienist license and look into permits. But first I just want to see how the energy in my house feels when I return. I think that's what I'm scared of most. What is that going to feel like? I'm just getting my normal sense of taste and smell back. I hope the smell of blood isn't in the air anymore. The fasten seat belt warning chimed alerting us to return to our seats. The captain let us know we were making our final descent and we'd experience some choppy air on the way down.

Then I thought about dealing with people again. I felt out of touch all of a sudden. I started thinking I wouldn't be relatable. What would my friends think of me, now? Would we still have anything in common? Would there be anything to talk about? What reality was I returning too? I gripped both of the armrests tightly. I had changed so much and I'm sure everyone else had done the same thing. I took a deep breath and got a grip of my imagination before stress tried to settle in. Chill Jason, you can do this man. I closed my eyes. The old white lady sitting next to me sensing my anxiety rubbed the top of my hand softly. It's going to be fine, dear; you don't have to be scared. It's just a little turbulence. She offered a sweet smile. I returned the expression, laughing to myself. Her statement was probably right on time. Okay then, God.

We landed safely, I collected Batty boy, my luggage, and debated whether to take a cab or the train home. It was Thursday just before lunch hour, and I didn't want to bother Mike to come all this way to get me. I really just wanted to ease into town and meet up with them at my leisure. I put Batman in his harness, collapsed his kennel, and secured it to my suitcase with the strap. I decided to take a cab home when I stepped outside and that "hawk" hit me.

I think I forgot how cold it gets. I didn't have a hat or gloves, but I had a hoodie I could throw on. My granny would be reading me to filth stepping out unprepared in this weather. I hailed a cab once I got my scene together. An old short black man popped out of the car with a flipped collar and a smile. He walked up to me introduced himself and gave my dog's head a few rubs. He then grabbed my bag and asked, "Say, young blood, where ya headed?" I gave him my address and he turned the heat in the car up. He joked about my lack of preparedness and we started talking about how Barack Obama could be the next president, ...if these white folks don't kill him. "I pray they don't mess with him, young blood... This what kids yo' age need to see, young blood... Oh I'm 69 years old, young blood... We had King, y'all gon' have Obama fo' yo' mama... So imagine seeing that... A Black President, from my home town, young blood... Shiiiiid! Ain't gon' be able to tell a nigga nuthin!"

A lot of the things he was talking about regarding Senator Barack Obama running for office I'd seen here and there on the island when I would call myself plugging back into the world through CNN. It was exciting passing by all the billboards and banners in support of this beautiful charismatic brotha with the slogan, "Yes We Can." I was proud that I lived here and that maybe I'd witness history step into good direction for a change. It would be dope for my niece to see a Black Man in the highest office of the land as a normal thing. If he could do something that brave, then my endeavor should be a breeze. It was kind of like I had entered a parallel universe. I felt like I was about to walk into something awesome. Now I couldn't wait to get home.

Mr. Sanders and I talked from the moment we left the airport curb until we reached my driveway. I had been gone for so long that everything looked like it was smaller than I remember. I stepped out of the car and Batman ran up into the yard to relieve himself. I got my stuff and headed up the walkway taking everything in. The grass looked like it had been taken care of and nothing looked out of the ordinary. I inhaled and went up the stairs to open the door. Batman was running around in circles in the front yard reacquainting himself with his territory. I laughed looking back at him have his fun. I got the door open and sat my bag in the foyer. My senses perked up when I heard noises that sounded like a muted tennis match.

RETURN

Someone was in my house. I let the screen door close quietly and readied one of the blades I carry. The groans got more rhythmic and got louder like either someone was fighting or fucking. As I continued to creep through the hall, I started to get an eye full. Michael butt naked on his back with some dark-skinned guy, riding his dick like his life depended on it. Imagine if Ciara really was a boy. He would give her a run for her money to redefine hump day. All this occurring on my brand-new couch! Pandora was playing a freak mix in the background. I stood in the doorway propped against the wall about half a minute before he realized I was there with my arms folded. His eyes got big and he tossed ol' boy to the side.

"Oh shit! Jason! Damn!" They scrambled to get their scene together. A flashback of Gee screaming, "Oh shit! Jason!" took me back to that night. I heard Batman scratching at the front door. I rolled my eyes and went to go and let him in out of the cold. After a quick hushed exchange of words, the guy he was with scurried into the bathroom.

"Come on, Batty boy," I said opening the door. He ran in and started jumping up on Mike's leg while he finished adjusting his sweats. I sucked my teeth, rolling my eyes at him when I walked into the living room. His semi erection was poking behind the light grey material, sitting low around his v-cut midsection. He looked like he had bulked up in the months that I was gone. He was rocking a bald head and beard cut close to his face.

"Jason, my bad, bae bro," he said smiling trying to explain and hug me at the same time. I could hear the water running in the bathroom. Michael was still moist with sexual perspiration.

"Really, Michael?" I said not the least bit surprised. However, I wasn't expecting to walk in on it. The image in my head kept replaying and was starting to piss me off. Batman ran to the bathroom door and started barking hysterically. I didn't stop him either.

"I know dis look real bad. It do. I know, but hea' me 'ot," he said grabbing my waist trying to charm with me that southern drawl. "I'm gon' make it up to you. I'm sorry, bae bro," he said looking me in the eyes.

"You just bought yourself a couch. I ain't sitting on that thing," I said pointing at it with the something stank face. You could still smell the sex in the air. And upon further investigation there was a bottle of chocolate sauce and a whipped cream can turned over on the floor. A bottle of lube was sitting on the table next to an empty golden ticket wrapper. I didn't want to know where the hell the condom was.

"I put a sheet over it. So it's all good. A lil' Resolve and Febreeze, we good," Mike smiled. I brushed his hands off of me sucking my teeth.

"Mike. I could see if it was a boyfriend I knew. Not saying that this or that would be okay. But why I got to come home to you and one of your ho's in my crib skeetin' nut on my new couch?" I said folding my arms.

"Your spot was convenient this time. This couch made the situation look sexy, and please don't call him a ho," Michael said with sincerity in his voice.

"Really?! Okay. BUST DOWN! Is he the delivery man, or some tea? I mean, he do got skills. Should I send him the invoice, seeing as you tipped him already? I mean can I RETURN it, or nah?!" I said yelling in the direction of the bathroom. I looked back at Mike. Batman was still barking.

"Ay! Chill 'ot!" he said shutting Batman down. Michael looked back at me. "And please, don't call him that either," he said with a somber look on his face.

"Since when did you start defending, BUST DOWNS!" I yelled again.

"Since he ain't no fuckin' bust down! Okay!" he said with a serious look on his face like I had done something wrong. That's when I realized this conversation was not even that serious. This was his typical behavior.

"Finish fucking, Michael," I said dismissively. He sucked his teeth loudly when I stopped in front of the bathroom door. Batman started growling. "Come help him get this nut, bruh! It's cool!" I looked back at Michael and winked. I gestured for him to continue, adjusted the thermostat, went upstairs to my room, and PAID IT!

RETURN

I unpacked, transferring most of the items in my suitcase onto the floor between the bathroom and my closet. I grabbed my phone and had Siri add, hamper, to the expanding list of things I needed to buy for the house. That was the area the dirty clothes used to be kept. I walked over to the window and peered out. The floor squealed from the pressure of my feet. The sound didn't remind me of Darius pacing this time. I sat on the window seal staring at the new bed and dresser. The two pieces looked different online, and I wasn't sure if I liked them either. My room looked and felt different. Kind of empty. That could be a good thing, seeing as I didn't want any freakin' reminders.

I tried to recall the events that took place in this space, but nothing would come to mind. I closed my eyes and took several deep breaths, holding onto one. I could hear my heartbeat. Batman's panting. The sound of the heat kicking on. The muffled sounds of the outside world. I exhaled, taking another breath to hold.

What was I doing back here. It felt and smelled sterile. Could I really do this? Can I live in this...house? This city? Chicago was me and...Gee. An image of pooling blood came to mind. I remember letting the soapy water soak the floor to loosen up the dried particles. I sat next to the puddle that day when I got the courage to clean it all up. I gazed at the red soapy water. The remnants of bloody notebook paper with dark ink lay suspended amidst the bubbles. Lurking, damn near taunting me. Read me! Reeeeaaad me! I was relieved when the Pine Sol and bleach finally overpowered the stench of death. Read me, BITCH! I could feel a tear well up in my eye. Darius' voice reverberated, "Fuck you, Jason!" The bedroom door swung open.

"Bae bro! You alright?" Michael said, knocking and entering at the same time. I snapped out of my solitude.

"Mm hm," I stood to my feet remembering to breathe. I removed my hoodie and t-shirt, tossing the garments onto the bare mattress.

"Ay, my bad you had to walk in on me in mid-session. I'm sorry, a'ight. Last thang I need to be doing right now is disrespectin' you and your house. Adding to your stress," he said being as sincere as possible. I untied my sneakers and carried them to the closet.

"Okay, Michael," I replied dryly, not really looking at him. I set the ironing board up and grabbed the iron from a box in the closet. I walked into the bathroom to freshen up. I turned the hot water on and wet a towel to wash my face.

"You mad at me?" he said walking up behind me, getting close locking his arms around me so I couldn't move. I sucked my teeth rolling my eyes at him when I caught his gaze in the mirror. He put his chin on my shoulder and gave me the puppy dog eyes, poking his perfectly shaped bottom lip out.

RETURN

"Mikie, you make me sick, man," I said bursting into laughter. "On my couch, though? Daaang!" He started laughing burying his face into my shoulder as he squeezed me tighter.

"I know right. I'm sorry," He said, looking up at me. "You fuh'gih me?" he said giving me the sad face again.

"Most people spill wine. Hell, maybe fart in the cushion to break one in, but not Mike," I said as we both started cracking up.

"I missed you, Jay! Damn it, man!" He started rocking me back and forth staring at my reflection in the mirror. He kissed my cheek.

"Ughhh, don't put your lips on me," I smiled, squinting my eyes as he kissed me again. "I missed your nasty butt too, man," I said rewetting the towel. I wrung it out and wiped my face down.

"How you feelin'? You good? Are you glad to be back?" he asked. He let the toilet rim down and popped a squat. I opened a bar of plain white soap and doused my face with water.

"I think so. I got to go and run some errands today," I said lathering up my face. "What are you doing up this way during the middle of the day. Aren't you supposed to be at work?"

"I'm on leave for the next couple of weeks."

"Oh, cool," I replied.

"And now that you're back, we got to celebrate the birthday boy. Saturday is the day! You ready, big booty?! We got a couple of surprises fo' dat ass!" he said smacking my butt.

"Yeah I guess so. I just want to be low key. Ain't nobody checkin for me, I'm sure," I said rinsing my face and turning off the water. I grabbed a towel to dry off, and then started brushing my teeth.

"You the talk of the town actually. Ery'time I go out, somebody asking about you. So, don't write yourself off jes' yet," Michael said. I finished up my oral hygiene and continued.

"We'll see," I chuckled. I put some moisturizer on my face and used the coil sponge on my hair. I stepped back into the closet to grab a shirt. Mike sat on the bed. "Thank you for putting my stuff away for me. That was sweet of you," I said returning with a purple polo to iron.

"You are welcome. Boy, you look incredible Jay, that Sun and shit did you some good bae bro! Look like that ass got phatter too," he joked. "Mmm mmm mmm."

"I know right, it probably did," I laughed, doing a quick twerk. I didn't do much but eat and workout. What's up with you and this bald Shamar Moore look you pulling off? I come back and every brotha in the city is rocking a beard," I smiled adjusting the shirt to iron the sleeves and collar.

"Blame that on Rick Ross," he laughed.

"Ma ma ma Maybach music," I said in a sexy feminine tone.

"Ricky got us lookin' mannish!" he said cheesing rubbing his face.

"I see! I ain't mad," I said smiling. I missed Michael and it was so good to see my brother.

"I got a shave profile from Medical for a personal compromise," he laughed. "I was starting to thin out in the corners, so I decided to do something about it before it really start showing. You like it?" he said caressing his scalp.

"It looks good on you!" I said taking a moment to give him a good once over. "You still got a cute thang happening," I continued.

"Awww, thanks, Jay," he said with this big Kool-Aid grin.

"That's what happens when you turn thirty," I warned. I switched the iron off and folded the board.

"Whatever! An' you right behind me, fool," he replied.

"As long as you go first," I chuckled.

"What you about to get into?" he asked.

"I'm about to get rid of the Bimmer. My Detroit connect put an Audi away for me, and I'm about to go see if I like it. If not I gonna find a used Prius or some tea," I said putting the iron and stuff up. I pulled the shirt over my body.

"A Prius my ass," he chuckled loudly. "What's wrong with the car you got?" Michael asked.

"It's attached to the past man, plus the front seats have these stains in it from the blood on Batman and the clothes I was wearing the night I had to go to the police station. I couldn't get the stains out of the leather on the passenger side. I don't want to ride around with that reminder every day," I said lacing up a pair of boots.

"I'm gon' go with you."

"Uh, don't you need to finish a bust down?" I said turning my nose up.

"He not a bust down, Jay," Michael laughed avoiding eye contact with me.

"You didn't finish?" I asked trying to keep a straight face.

"He took the train home, fool," he smiled.

"Hurry up, Michael," I said rolling my eyes. "I need to walk and feed Batman before I go anyway. Come on, Batty boy," I said as we walked out of my bedroom.

"I'm saying, though," he said still laughing. He grabbed me and pulled me close to him with his phone extended out with FaceTime chiming.

"Jason! Oh my gosh, sweetie! You grew your hair out! Welcome back!" Preston yelled. "Shawn, come here! Jason is back!" He screamed just as Shawn ran up and got in the screen.

RETURN

"You know, they roommates, now," Michael whispered to me.

"Whaaaat?" I mouthed silently. Michael shook his head yes mouthing the words, we'll talk.

"Hey, WHORE! Come on hair! Yesss!" Shawn screeched as Michael laughed rubbing my hair.

"Hey, hags! You like it?" I said laughing at the two of them.

"I do! Happy Birthday, queen! You ready to cut up, WHORE!" Shawn screeched. "Bitch, you know we takin' you to...a Ooooph!" Preston ran and grabbed the phone from him shutting his mouth in the process as I laughed.

"Ah, ah! Put Shawn back on the phone, where we going?" I asked laughing at the two of them fighting.

"We'll catch up with ya'll!" Michael said laughing.

"Bye, Jason and Mikie!" He looked over at Shawn. Bitch! You know you can't ho..." Preston said ending the call.

And just like that, I felt like everything was going to be alright. I was back home with my family. Maybe I was right where I belonged. Maybe it was the right time to be here. This time...

BAE

We couldn't all get together Wednesday night like we wanted to, so we settled on Saturday. Maseo was straight this month, and he damn near threatened our homegirl Stella the fella to get us into this swanky ass strip club near Evanston called MainStage. It's supposed to be the best in the Midwest. She got us a hook-up for the VIP back room through some girl she scissored. She say that's where the celebrities and ballers go. It was going to be me, Mase, Dave, and Steal. We grew up with her lil' womanizing ass. Her nickname is "Steal'ya" as in she'll steal ya girl. She snagged a bad one from Dave this one time, which is hard to do. But she's bagged several from Maseo's pretty boy ass. They still play the number gettin' in the summer game. It was a tie this past year. I copped some singles and headed upstairs to Dave's to pregame before we all rolled out to the night spot.

I had been to strip clubs before with my niggas. It's one of Stella's favorite things to do, next to cheifin', and Giordano's. It's not my favorite, but it didn't really bother me. I like to flirt with females anyway. The shit's fun. It's nothing spectacular, just an interesting environment to socialize in. I remember the first time I went with them. For shits and giggles. Stella was schooling, If the girl on stage know what she doing, she can change the atmosphere. Some of these girls man, got heaven and Earth between their thighs. Steal said many of 'em don't know they worth. Givin' it up to two buck Chuck.

But if she know what she doing. How to work that nigga mind. The ass is just a rattle to a man. A toy to play with. I've seen niggas' lose houses, spreading the mortgage across the pussy panty line. Them the ones that ain't got to fuck to get what she want. I don't know what it's like to be a female, but living with the women in my family, I know what power they possess. Maybe that's why Mom never looked for another worthy opponent. I never asked her why either. But here we are at the titty bar. And it is impressive. I don't smell pussy, smoke, Axe, or, Old Spice. Good lighting. Sturdy structure. Sound insulation? I could help them with the acoustics. They could do better. I got to remind myself to leave my card, I thought as one of the pretty shapelier sistas twerked her way by carrying a huge round of drinks. The waitresses had on African print covering the pum-pum's.

The drinks are strong, and I'm sky diving. Impressed. Black owned and operated. Music to my ears. And so far, the customer service is tolerable. I felt I could relax. We had a booth with this crazy fly view of the main stage. The show hadn't started yet and there were a couple more booths they were getting ready to fill. One of the waitresses started dancing on me after she brought our drinks to us. I was in my weed, feeling my moment. Head bobbing to the motion of the booty in my face. Stella, was up dancing and sipping on her drink. Mase and Dave were conversatin' about Michelle Obama when they decided to clown.

"Nigga, that's bae right there," Maseo said ribbing Dave. They both started staring at me. Looking goofy an' shit.

"Pen can't handle all that, look at his face, my dude," Dave answered. Both they asses were high as fuck. Squinting. "Look at his face!" She made her way over to grind with Stella.

"What the fuck is bae?" I said laughing, as the next song blended in. Stella tipped the girl. She kissed Stella on the cheek and went back to work.

"That's what these niggas is calling these silly ho's these days, bro. Bae. Like how nigga's used to be like wifey," Stella said. "Short for baby, possibly the one, my top bitch. Bae is the new boo," she smiled.

"How do you not know that?" Dave asked.

"Cause he secretly looking for a Carlton Banks type, fuck you tal'bout?" Stella said. Dave and her ass fell into each other laughing.

"Pen, man, you in the Chi, not a E. Lynn Harris book. You gon' have to lower these standards a little bit man. I mean, you ain't gotta keep fuckin' with the trash you been fuckin' with. But be realistic about these fuckin' nigga-spectations. Everybody can't be Raymond," Maseo said trying to sound like he was speaking gospel not jealousy. I chuckled to myself holding his gaze.

"Keep waiting for it, nigga," I laughed. Bobbing my head. Sipping my beer.

"Waitin'? For what?" he asked, all dead ass.

"To durb my dick," I said. Maseo had a paranoid look on his face all of a sudden. I caught him off guard. I smiled peeping the look on Dave's face.

"Who's E. Lynn Harris and Raymond?" Dave asked. Me and Maseo looked at each other and cracked up.

"Yo, I'm dead ass! How you not know that hanging around these two niggas?" Stella laughed tossing her locks back. She rolled her eyes and Maseo gave her a pound.

"I mean, shit! I ain't gay," he laughed shrugging his shoulders.

"What you gon' say, Dave?" I laughed taking a sip of my beer. "Y'all on this shit again, man?" I said looking away.

"Yo' we just concerned, bro! I mean, shit, yo' own mommy sent you on a trip to go get some," Dave said.

"That ain't why she sent me..." I stopped talking once I realized all they asses had the "nigga please" look on they faces.

"A boyfriend might do your high-strung arrogant ass some good, P," he continued with a shoulder shrug.

"So that's why we here, Mase? Y'all niggas trying to turn me out?" I joked.

"That ain't the reason we here," he said looking at Dave weird as fuck. Stella smirked lighting up a blunt she rolled in the parking lot.

"Man, no. You asked what bae was and somehow, no disrespect, we ended up in agreement with Ms. Reign. You need one. You spend too much time on them houses, man. And by yourself. And quite frankly, dawg," he said looking at Stella and Maseo, "I know she's your heart. And I know that's your livelihood, but Pen, I do your books. You got your Mom living comfortable. You can slow down just a tad to live some of your life. For you. You been working your ass off since middle school. Chill. The. Fuck. Out. You missed out on your teens and your twenties. Don't do the same in your thirties, P." Dave said with that fatherly advice he always seems to fuckin' have. He can always drop a load on you and keep it pushing. I looked at 'em for a minute. I snatched the blunt from Stella's fingertips. Took two pulls. Passed it to Dave. Nodded my head.

"I'm bought to go piss," I said getting up to walk away. I stopped. "Do I need a man for that too?"

"Pen, man, don't trip," Maseo pleaded. He almost got my arm in his hand. I snatched away.

"You just...! Don't fuck up the rotation. Blowing my high ass niggas," I fired back trying not to be hood and loud.

"Let him go cool off, Mase, he'll be alright," I heard Dave spew in the background.

The room was now full, and the energy had definitely picked up as the MC announced the girls would be hitting the main stage in five minutes. The waitresses were doing they thang. Shaking ass and keeping the liquor flowing, priming us up for the main dishes. I walked to the bathroom to handle business. I pissed, stepped out the stall, and to a sink to wash my hands. No one was there. I took a long look at myself in the mirror.

I got over my prideful embarrassment. I was getting over the fact that Mom had a point. I was just tired of hearing everybody tell me what I need. I hate to admit they're right. I don't want to pick the wrong nigga, though. Like Mom. And I don't want to hurt nobody. Like dad. Sex is easy. A quick easy cop out. Its cost effective emotionally but had become routine. Something to do to check off a requirement of time spent with a warm body. It's a microwave version of emotional attachment. Getting close, but not close enough. Pointless sex. No cigarette. Who cares if it's good for him long as it's wet.

This obvious gay dude walked into the bathroom. He was wearing all black with large pink sun glasses, a pink pair of Tim's, and a pink female sport coat. He had on one of those paper cone birthday hats. He paused and flinched when he noticed me. He smiled and tip-toed into a stall. I heard the door lock. I chuckled shaking my head and went back into the party. On my way, I passed by a booth housing a few cuties doing the Stanky Legg with a couple of the waitresses. They were each wearing a birthday hat like the lil' guy in the bathroom, so I assumed they were all together. I got back to the table just in time for my turn on the blunt.

"We good, P?" Dave asked, smiling putting me in a head lock when I sat down.

"Yeah, man. We family, now get yo' big ass off me," I laughed adjusting my fitted as Maseo took the tree. He laughed and coughed a lil' smoke out.

"Just making sure," he said as Stella shook her head. The lights dimmed as the MC started the show with Luke playing softly in the background...

"Good evening ladies and gentlemen. Welcome to the MainStage VIP suite. If you've never been here before. You're in store for so much more than your average hood whore store can offer. Our women are queens. We ask that you treat them as such. We ask that you act like gentlemen so that everyone can have the erotic experience of a lifetime. If she say NO! Please do not touch! My warning is your final warning. We don't mind if you smoke. Be responsible. We definitely don't mind if you drink. Again, be responsible. We're about to start it off nice, slow, and sexy with a bevy of ladies rocking a sexy lingerie line from Chicago's very own, upcoming Project Runway contestant, Preston! Congratulations to you young brotha! Fellas! I seen the girls a minute ago, and mannnnnn....! That's all I'm gonna say! Tip these ladies, tip these waitresses, and buy them dranks! The ladies 'bout to make it wet, sexy, and freaky..."

After he shut up, the brothas with the birthday hats started cheering and clapping for the guy in the pink. He must be Preston. He stood up to take a bow. I took another hit of the blunt and passed it. I grabbed my beer and leaned back with my foot propped up on the table. The lights started to go up as the girls came out to, Trina. They started out in black trench coats teasing the crowd. The one in the pink had Stella's attention once that coat hit the floor.

"Ooooo, look at the one in the pink! That bitch thicker than a Snicker, dawg! I'm bagging that tonight," she said heading up to the stage with a stack of ones. "Finish this," she handed me the blunt. Maseo got up to join her. Giggling and shit.

"Pen, we just love you bro, a'ight. You can't take love personal." Dave said. I took a pull of the blunt and passed it to him.

"I know, Dave," I said smilin' my ass off.

"I just want you to be happy," he said as the guys with the Pink Panther started getting a little rowdy. I couldn't believe my eyes. The MC made an announcement that the girls were going to cater to the birthday boy in the audience.

"OH?!" I said with my eyes wide as fuck.

"Nigga! What?" Dave asked looking around.

"Bro' that's bae," I said tapping him in the chest. Pointing towards the stage. I sat up like the teacher called me out. I couldn't fuckin' believe it.

"Who you pointing at? Mase, bum ass? Fuck you tal'bout?" Dave asked, looking at me with confusion. He passed me the blunt.

"Lil' daddy right there. That's bae," I said looking at Dave, who adjusted his glasses and nodded his head looking back at me.

"Okay, just to be clear. Not the one with that pink shit on?"

"Nah! Da one on the stage, Dave. Birthday boy," I said cheesing like a motherfucka! Something in my stomach flipped. Swear to God.

"OH?! He's a sharp lookin', brotha! You act like you know him, or nah?" Dave asked. He finished his drink.

"That's the crazy part. I think I do. I can't remember from where though. I bumped into him at the airport on the way back home. He was on my same flight and shit. Now he here," I said scratching my head. He was looking right. He had on a red button-down fitted to his body and another pair of expensive looking jeans huggin' on the phattness. His birthday hat was different from everybody else's.

"You sure he gay. I mean, he look quite comfy up there. Like he enjoying the show more than Stella, damn. I can't tell," Dave said laughing. His friends were cheering him on around the stage dancing and making it rain. His lil' turn up was fyre.

"That lil' nigga fine as fuck, Dave. Shit!" I said rubbing my face. The weed had me on one. I had to shoot my shot again.

"Alright! Well, go say something to him. He don't look girly at least, or is that what you like? No judgement. I'm just saying, I just don't see you with no punk, you know what I'm saying. Like, a soft, floaty, gay dude, you know?" Dave rambled on, trying hard not to be offensive. I knew what he meant.

"This one is different. I gotta even out first, before I say something," I said staring at him, taking a long gulp of beer. I was faded, but aware of my target. I finished the last bit of the satin. "This some good shit."

"Right?! Steal got that from Keisha, up the street, who got that from Roe off of Stoney," he said looking at the nearest female booty in view.

"Smokin' on keesha!" I laughed.

"Say dawg. Is you gon' get at birthday boy, or nah?" Dave asked, killing me with these questions.

"Yeah, I'm definitely doin'nat," I said cheesing. But how though? What to say, though? I had to chill. My heart was starting to race.

"Nigga, what you blushing and shit for? What y'all talkin' about Dave?" Maseo asked as he and Stella came back to the table.

"He think he found, bae," Dave said tapping Maseo in the chest. He cracked up!

"What!? You see the light all of a sudden, or naw? Where bae, at? Point this bitch out! I'm like Aaliyah, nigga, let me know," he joked. Him and Stella both cracked up.

"See the sharp looking dude in the red shirt," Dave said pulling him in close to point him in the right direction. Maseo pulled Dave's glasses off pretending to look through 'em.

"OH?! Da Birf'day boy! Damn. That's bae!? Yeah, up close he a good look. I like his hair too. Nigga, I saw him first, so whassup?" Maseo said, handing Dave his glasses back.

"Go get him, Mase. Pen square ass ain't gon' say shit. He scared of the cute ones," Stella teased licking her thumb. She started counting off another stack of singles.

"He damn sure is," Maseo said calling my bluff. He was hawking 'em.

"I'm sure it's a hood rat among them, he'll choose. You know, the easy prey," Stella laughed.

"Low hanging fruit loving ass nigga," Maseo said snickering giving me the treatment.

BAE

"I don't know, y'all. He just might, he perked the fuck up when he saw him. Said he peeped him in the airport," Dave said.

"OH?!" Maseo and Stella said in unison. That was our shit either to instigate some bullshit or emphasis some real shit or for whenever appropriate.

"Fuckin' really?" Stella asked.

"And on the plane back home, Steal," Dave added. He was smiling and nodding his head to the beat finally getting the attention of our waitress. She was speaking to the mystery guys party. She let him know she'd be a minute.

"Nigga, put that on er'ythang? Dead ass! He was on the plane with you?" Maseo asked. His eyes were chinky as hell, and he had that goofy smile on his face that made us all laugh when he was good and stoned.

"True story. In first class," I said looking over at Maseo. Then back at "bae." He was jukin' to the beat. This pretty ass light skinned nigga grabbed him and started pawing at him. He pulled him close whispering something in his ear. He inched closer laughing. I assumed that must be the nigga he talking too. The one he snubbed me for. Hmm. A challenge. I got a little salty wishing that was me speaking, Come ride shotgun Lil' daddy, in his ear.

"And nigga, you ain't upgrade?! PEN! You got till midnight, or I swear I'm hittin' that ass tonight. Birf'day dick! Birf'day dick!" he started singing like Jermih. "I'm pullin' them twists and er'ything," Maseo said with a straight face staring at they table.

"His hair was sexy ass fuck, Pen," Stella said nodding her head instigatin' and shit. Maseo was still rambling.

"Dogging that shit the fuck out. Da booty pro'ly good as fuck too. I'ma be hittin' it from the back, pullin' them twists, like. Uggnnh! Ugnnnh! Ugnnnnh! UGHHHH!" Maseo kept talking his shit.

"I love a bitch with her natural hair. Ain't nothing sexier," Stella added.

"Have them legs crimped back. Sitting pretty right on my shoulders next," Maseo said fucking with me. "Just tagging that shit. He gon' be moanin' my name and shit. Then, I'm gon' have my dick brushin' them tonsils, right. Have him durbin' my shit like, Gargle my name bae! Gargle that shit nigga! Yeah, he proba..."

"Shut the fuck up, Mase!" Dave said with his face all twisted up. "Damn! You's a ig'nant ass!"

"Clocks ticking, nigga. Actually, it's a couple cuties over there. But I do like, uhhh, yeah. I like bae the most," Maseo said bobbing his head slow. That nigga know he be trying to get up under my skin. He pulled a money click from his pocket. Holding my gaze.

"Aww, don't do it to him, Mase," Stella said.

"I'm gon' help you pay to get it home." He laid a Grant down and looked over at "bae's" table licking his chops.

"And there it is," Stella pointed at the table.

BAE

"I see you brought a little pocket change from your closet," I smiled finishing my beer.

"These niggas," she said rolling her eyes. Then pulled a fiddy from the tiddy. Tossed it down. Leaned back like a G' with her grill showing. Arms folded. "He look 'spainsive. Filet Mignon type, cutie. Them be the freaks."

"Come on y'all, he said that's bae. We can't bet on, bae. Can we?" Dave said trying to be fucking Switzerland. He know he wanted in on this. The bet to see if I'd shoot my shot with the quote unquote unattainable pretty boy. My kryptonite. The stakes was high tonight showcasing our respective balls. We been like this since we started workin' summer jobs back in the day. Bettin' on some bullshit.

"Obama said, Yes we can," Maseo laughed. The pressure was on. But I was down. I'll be damned if I let Maseo ho ass follow through, with a storyline tomorrow. But judging by lite brite in cutie's booth, Maseo might be more his move.

"If he bae, step to him, bag that ass tonight, and tell us what you think in the morning. This just a little added incentive to see if he out of your league. Whaddup doe, Pen?" Stella said.

"He ain't bae, if he don't stay past noon. You in this shit Dave, or naw?" Maseo asked. Dead ass.

"For the record, this is stupid but fuck it. Let's see if he bae. Shoot the jay, P!" Dave peeled off two $20's and a $10.

"Shoot it!" Sat the bills down and looked at me after pretending to shoot a free-throw. They all looked at me. I looked over at my target posted up. Looking like a buttery brown wet dream I've had. I weighed my odds and I thought back to my airport brick. Our waitress came back to the table. She had a bucket with four bottles of Guinness on ice. She placed it in the middle of the table. There was one frosty mug that she put in front of me. She popped the top off one of the bottles and served only me.

"This is compliments of the birthday boy in suite number 8. He says to tell Pen hello. Enjoy, handsome!" she said. She gave my forearm a couple of squeezes winking at me as she put a switch in them hips.

"OH?!" Dave and Stella said staring at me like cartoons.

They grabbed a bottle each and gave one another a clink of the glass. Mase had a salty look on his face like it should have been him. I played it cool. I had my in. I rubbed my beard thinking, *he get mad cool points for the round.* I felt like King Dingaling. Nigga! For me and my dawgs?! Shit got my dick kind of hard. He baited the fuck out of the hook. I peeped him popping that sexy ass. That's when I locked eyes with bae. I grabbed my mug then the loot. My loot. Soon I'd be grabbing that booty. My prize. I held his gaze. I smiled. Gave him the nod. Motioned for him to meet me on the patio. Let the hunt commence...

TITI'S

I used to moonlight for Graham Dental and Associates when I first started out in Chicago after my Navy days. Dr. Graham took a chance on me placing me under his wing after I separated from service. He helped me to fine-tuned the things I learned in school as a hygienist, and what the Navy taught me as a Tech. He was focused. He was stern and expected nothing but polished excellence from his staff. He had a couple of locations to serve various parts of the city and I like that he wasn't discriminatory in his delivery.

The flagship practice he owned was a modest size facility located near downtown off of E. Washington and N. Wabash. It was a great place to work and expand the scope of my functions under his license. I logged a lot of long hours there meeting all sorts of people, building a reliable clientele, and talking about all things black with Susan. She was the widowed receptionist that kept the place humming on all eight cylinders, especially during his frequent extended hour weekdays.

After Gary died, I started working there full-time declining a less strenuous job offer on the Naval base. 7AM to 3PM 8 patients a day, would have been cake. However, working for Dr. Graham, I'd be able to make more money, which afforded me the opportunity to stay in the city. Work was all I knew up until I left for the

Bahamas last year. A butt load of time went by and it's like I almost didn't miss a beat, instantly putting things back in order. I replaced a bunch of necessary items I felt were missing to make this house a home. Michael has been crashing here and helping me out by being a welcomed nuisance. The last couple days has found me assembling this and that or flying up the Ike in the middle of the night to the 24-hour Walmart in Schaumburg for something I needed. Honestly, any excuse for me to drive my new sports car was my other reason. I was excited about my life again.

I got a call from Susan this morning telling me that Dr. Graham wanted me to meet him at the office to discuss a matter of great importance before he went out of town on his winter vacation. I reluctantly agreed to meet them early, even though I was planning to sleep in. Now that the house was almost assembled to my liking, I was preparing to be kidnapped by my crew. They were more excited about my birthday than I was. Birthdays have never been a big deal to me. I mean, I celebrate other folks birthdays, but I like to keep mine low key and junk. Something simple like reflecting over a cupcake and catching a show. Mama is big on birthdays too and I used to pretend for her sake. But I was giddy about celebrating this year. I was up, earlier than I wanted to be, imagining what Michael, Shawn, and Preston had cooked up. They are all different variations of Virgo, so birthdays for them are celebrated the whole freakin' month. With my return, I was in for something major, I'm sure.

I made the mistake of letting Batman sleep in the bed with me on the island, so here he was knocked out right up under me. He barely moved as I got out of bed and made my way into the bathroom to relieve myself and brush my teeth. I decided I'd try to squeeze a run in before I met with doc, but remembered I wasn't on the beach anymore, and it was too cold for that crap. I needed to come up with a contingency plan where that was concerned. I jumped in the shower, got my scene together, and headed downstairs to walk and feed the dog.

Michael was knocked out tucked away like a baby, looking all adorable with drool starting to ooze from his mouth. He made himself at home on the new sofa I watched him disinfect under my close OCD supervision. I still can't say for sure if I'd be satisfied with any result judging by the image imprinted on my frontal lobe, though. We'll roll with it for the sake of a recap. I decided to send him a text that I'd be back. I put Batty boy in his cage with some water, grabbed a coat and gloves, and walked out to the car.

When I stepped into the garage and the light hit my new silver toy, kitted out, sitting pretty with the 19's on low profiles, my smile spread East to West. Merch from the D' did me right this time. He's the connect that Andre uses and put me on to a while back. He's a legit car enthusiast with a legit operation called Windy City Imports. He sold me my last couple of cars.

"Happy birthday, bae bro!" Michael said coming in yawning and smiling. He threw his arm around my neck.

"Aww thanks," I said giggling.

"Jay, dis, shit sexy as fuck on you, bae bro! What old dude called it again?"

"Boy oh, boy! Do I got a beautiful set of titties for you to play with, Mr. Williams!" I said rubbing my hands together and pretending to motorboat a set. I was imitating my sales guy.

"The titties!" Michael said laughing. "The look on your face was fuckin' priceless."

"The TT-S, crazy," I said bursting into laughter.

"It's tight. I can't believe you didn't get a stick shift?" he said.

"I know, right! It only come with a dual clutch trans, probably because of the new Quattro system. It's got the paddles, though," I replied folding my arms.

"Only yo' ass could pull this shit off right here. I like it Jay! Look at God!" Michael said peering inside.

"Yes, sir, you need to let Merch get you out of that Lac' and behind the wheel of a quality automobile!" I joked imitating him again. I walked over to the driver's side of the car.

"I might see what he talkin' if its 'bout a new Cadillac,"

"Of course," I said rolling my eyes getting inside. "I'll be back." I buckled up and pressed the red button to start the car. I smiled at the burble from the exhaust note.

"Way'ment! Where you going? Walmart again?" Michael said as I revved the engine and opened the garage door. He stuffed his hands in his sweats and walked back inside while I backed out of the driveway.

He called me and threatened me not to be gone long since he had a strategic itinerary laid out for me today. I'm try'na maximize the day, shawty! Don't be out slow pokin'! I told him not to worry and that I'd be back as soon as possible. I took the inbound Kennedy to the Loop, zipping through the cold empty weekend streets. The sleeping giant was still laying low as the sun burst through the grey clouds in sporadic intervals. Steam wafted through the makeshift nostrils of the man hole covers. I passed by a group of people with Barack the Vote signs inspiring people to register to vote. Seeing a brotha from Chicago run for President was one of the most phenomenal things to witness in person. I wonder if communities rallied around Shirley Chisolm and Rev. Jesse Jackson when they did the same. This election represents so many things for so many people. Plus his wife and kids are black like me; I was all in. I speak in faith and say, when he wins, I hope he actually stands up to the much-needed expectations placed on his candidacy.

I pulled into the underground parking deck of the Dental Office and bundled up. Only two other spaces were filled, which at this hour on a Saturday for Dr. Graham, was odd. I took the elevators up to the main level and walked towards the empty reception area. Susan was sitting quietly at the front desk with a magazine facing a gorgeous view of the city. Once she heard me come through the door, she turned, and her face lit up.

"Oh my goodness! Jason! Look at my baby!" she said stepping from around the desk as quickly as she could in her high heel shoes. She had her hair styled in loose curls sitting over her shoulder. Definitely out of her norm.

"What's going on, kissy missy?" I said. I called her that because she always kissed folks on the cheek when she greeted them. I reached out to meet her embrace.

"How are you doing, young man? Look at you? I like this new natural hair thing you got going on. This is cute on you Jason! Hmph!" she said squeezing the life out of me and kissing my cheek right on queue. I laughed to myself, as she let me go.

"Thank you. I'm doing fine, I love these curls, Sue!" I said blushing. "How you doing?" I asked. She leaned back on the desk.

"Oh, I'm well. I hear someone has a birthday today," she said smiling. "How old are you now?"

"Yes, ma'am, I turn 28 today," I smiled proudly.

"Okay, so today is your actual birthdate?" she asked grabbing the remote to mute the TV.

"Yes, ma'am. Today is the day," I replied.

"Don't you start with the ma'am mess with me, Jason. I'm older than you but not by much," she said tapping my shoulder.

"I'll do my best," I winked. "So what, y'all closed on Saturdays now? Why so empty?" I asked looking around. It was odd not hearing the sound of the CNN, the phone ringing, or the whistling turbines of the handpieces drilling away.

"Jimmy is with a patient right now. A little girl fell chasing after the family dog this morning and cracked a couple of teeth. When he's done, he'll explain why it's so empty in here," she said winking at me.

"Aww, is she alright?" I asked concerned.

"Yeah! She's a fat shy little thing. With her little crocodile tears. She reached way down to the bottom of my candy jar for the biggest sucker she could find. Bless her heart, Lord. Literally," Susan said laughing waving her hand in the air like she was swatting a fly away.

"You are still a sweet mess," I chuckled. "Okay, since when are we on a first name basis with, Jimmy?" I said teasing and pointing at her before I started laughing.

"That's the other part."

"What part?" I asked.

"This part." She held her left hand out displaying what any woman would call an, exquisitely blinged out engagement ring. I grabbed her hand pulling her in close.

"Whaaaat!? Congratulations! Oh my God, lady! When did this all happen?" I asked giving her hand a squeeze before letting it go.

"It started over this low-cut shirt Donna said I should wear. She said he was talking about how pretty my skin was, and she saw something in his eye. She suggested I show a little more skin. So I did," she blushed giggling like a school girl.

"Jezebel," I winked.

"Nothing too revealing, but enough to keep his attention. She did my hair and put a little make up on me in the mornings, and he asked me out to dinner one day. He was so sweet and made me feel like a lady again. We went out more and more, and two months ago. TA DAAA!" She said holding up her hand admiring her ring.

"I knew he liked a little mocha in his skim milk. He was always more personable with the sistas that come in here."

You gon' head then, Susan!" I said just as Dr. Graham walked in to escort the patient and her mother up to the front. They exchanged pleasantries, and she congratulated him on his engagement and his retirement.

"Jason Williams! The man of the hour," he said walking up to kiss Susan. "Hey beautiful," he said making her blush.

"How you doing, doc?" I smiled.

"Did she tell you the news?" he asked patting my shoulder.

"Yeah, she's pregnant, right?" I said joking with a puzzled look on my face. They broke out into laughter.

"They say that's next, the baby carriage, huh? What do you say?" He winked at her giving her a come-hither look.

"I'm done raising babies, and so is this one," she laughed pointing a thumb at him.

"Yeah, she told me. Congratulations you two!" I mused. They looked so happy and I was happy for them. Susan especially. She was an amazing woman that deserved someone special.

"No. Not that news. The retirement news," he said. I was happy for him but thought what did that have to do with me coming to the office on my birthday.

"Oh, congratulations again! Are you guys running off to Boca Raton or the French Riviera. I hear dentists retire in those two places."

"I have family in Boca, but we won't be spending our days there with them. That's not on the road course," he laughed. I looked over at Susan, who was squinting her eyes and shaking her head.

"Oh Lord, the Winnebago tour! He got you onboard his Winnie and the Boo dream?" I said bursting into laughter along with Susan.

"Oh come on guys! It's one of America's last great adventures. RV'ing. Hitting the open road. Getting our kicks on old Route 66." He embraced Susan and kissed her forehead. "The woman of my dreams finally on my arm. Huh? Come on," he said, shrugging his shoulders with his arms out smiling as if he just pitched a good sale.

"I picked out the RV," Susan said hanging her head as I started laughing hysterically. She used to clown doc for this idea, and she ended up being the "boo."

"My, my, my! Looks like Jesus won't be the only co-pilot," I joked.

"Oh, Jimmy, get to the point so this boy can enjoy getting OLD!" she said looking at me with a scowl on her face. She stuck her tongue out at me. We all laughed for a second before doc started up again.

"I'll make this quick. Jason, that idea you were cooking up a while back. Did you ever come up with that model and business plan I kept hounding you about?" he asked placing his hands behind his back. Susan stood by with a serious look on her face all of a sudden. She gave him a quick glance.

"Yes. I have a plan I sketched out," I said not sure if what I came up with would hold a candle to what I think his idea of a business model would look like. I also knew first-hand how he ran his business.

"Good. Because my future wife and I," he paused for affect looking at Susan who was now smiling at me, "have decided to sell the Westview office to Dr. Montano. The Northside office will be sold to Dr. Wilshire. And we would like to give you this clinic to open up your very own hygiene practice. If you're interested. What do you say? Huh?" he said as Susan let out a nervous giggle. I was in shock when I realized what he said.

"Wait, give me. You're giving me a whole clinic, doc?" I asked as my heart started to skip some beats.

"WE! Thought it would be no one better to hand it off too," he smiled looking at Susan. She dangled a ring of keys in front of me. I was in awe looking around with my hand covering my mouth.

"Well, what do you say, child? This is the birthday gift I was telling you about," she said grabbing my hands. Tears welled up in my eyes.

"HELL YES! Thank you!" I said shouting to the moon with tears streaming down my face as I looked down at the keys in my right hand. Life was paying me back for something I must have done right. I couldn't control my joy as Susan wrapped her arms around me. Beauty for ashes.

"It's a big responsibility, so hire yourself a good lawyer, let's fine tune your plan, and draw up some paperwork," he said walking over to shake my hand. I gripped it tightly, and he pulled me in close. "You earned it, buddy. Congratulations!" he said as Susan dabbed my face with Kleenex.

After I left Dr. Graham's office. Excuse me, after I left my office. I went to grab a quick mix from Garret's Popcorn and headed home with the outstanding news. My head was still reeling in the excitement of what just happened. Never in a million years did I think someone would just hand me the keys to my own clinic without me having to do the legwork. This one blessing alleviated so much stress and opens up so many more opportunities for me than I imagined. Whatever the night was going to bring I was totally up for it.

When I got home, Shawn had arrived. Michael gave me just enough time to walk and feed my dog, enjoy my treat, and get a good kee-kee in, before they blindfolded me, and whisked me off to unknown places for the so-called star treatment. We went and got my hair cut first, followed by mani-pedi's, which is when I got the tea about Shawn while he was on his phone outside. So, apparently him and Andre broke up a couple months ago because of Shawn's recent strange behavior. The last straw was when Shawn accused Dre of sleeping with me or at least wanting to when my name kept coming up in conversation. Especially when asked of his whereabouts and why he spent so much time with me before I left for the Caribbean. Shawn made a scene in the lobby windmilling Dre after a couple nights of binging off of some drug. Dre put him out saying, "Maybe I picked the wrong friend, cause Gary lucked out that night in Atlanta."

Upon further investigation, Shawn had started hanging out with this grimy dude who Michael think got the boy using from time to time. His usual over the top personality was an unpredictable nightmare these days. They weren't sure which Shawn was going to appear each time they hung out. Preston took him in to help get his scene together, but that situation may not last because Preston was going to be packing up his life, hopefully not temporarily, to move to LA to shoot Project Runway. My boys hard work and grind towards his dream finally paid off. He was due to leave the end of February and put together a celebratory showcase of a lingerie line he came up with over the last few months, to test out his results. All I know was that it was going to be held at some spot called the MainStage. My gut was telling me to google it, but I forgot about the mental note I made when the girl worked her magic on my feet.

The next stop brought us back to my crib so that we could get ready for the main event. Preston was supposed to come and pick us all up at some point. A couple of folks we knew from hanging out came by to join the festivities. We were drinking, dancing, and having a good time when later that night, Michael got a call letting him know a Party

Bus was parked outside ready to take us to our next destination.

When we got downstairs, Preston popped through the door revealing a decked-out bus with a DJ, mini bar, a male and female stripper, complete with individual poles. Michael joked with me about being indoctrinated into manhood as he put the blindfold back on me when the bus got closer to the location. A doggone female strip club near Evanston. I should have known better but went with the flow. I warned Michael if a titty came anywhere near my lips, a broad was getting punched in the chest.

The place was really nice. Not what I expected at all. It was clean and the waitresses were gorgeous. I could only imagine what the main girls looked like. The cool part was they had black girls of all sizes. Preston says he had a few classes with a girl he knew from the Art Institute. Working at MainStage was how she paid her tuition and then some. She's still doing it from time to time until her dream as a designer pops off. She was one of the girls kicking off the show in his Lingerie line. I couldn't wait to see what he came up with. I especially couldn't wait to see what the strip club hype was all about.

There were some good-looking guys in the different VIP booths as well. Each booth, or suite as they called them, had its own plush theme that wasn't gaudy. So far, I was having a good time. I went back stage with Preston so that he could check on the girls and make adjustments before they hit the stage. They were just supposed to dance in these outfits, not strip, he reminded them. This was just a teaser before the nakedness, I guess. Once he was satisfied, we hurried back to our booth and he signaled the MC to start the show.

"Good evening ladies and gentlemen. Welcome to the MainStage VIP suite. If you've never been here before. You're in store for so much more than your average hood whore store can offer. Our women are queens. We ask that you treat them as such. We ask that you act like gentlemen so that everyone can have the erotic experience of a lifetime. If she say NO! Please do not touch! My warning is your final warning. We don't mind if you smoke. Be responsible. We definitely don't mind if you drink. Again, be responsible. We're about to start it off nice, slow, and sexy with a bevy of ladies rocking a sexy lingerie line from Chicago's very own, upcoming Project Runway contestant, Preston! Congratulations to you young brotha! Fella's! I seen the girls a minute ago, and mannnnnn....! That's all I'm gonna say! Tip these ladies, tip these waitresses, and buy them dranks! The ladies 'bout to make it wet, sexy, and freaky..."

"Congratulations, Preston!!" Our party started cheering him on and shouting and chanting like we were on the Arsenio Hall show. He got up to take a bow as the lights dimmed. We all got hype again as these beautiful girls came out bouncing to "Baddest Bitch" by Trina. They had black trench coats on at first and when they took the coats off, one of them snuck down with a carrot cupcake that had a lit sparkler on top. She sat it in front of me and pulled me up onto the stage. Next thing you know I had eight sets of titties and ass at my disposal. I was having a ball dancing with the girls and feeling the softness of their curves rub and caress my skin. They made it a fun and worthwhile experience, especially with the help of my girl Trina spitting some prime game if you listen to the lyrics carefully.

While I was on stage, I got a good view of the crowd. Folks were enjoying themselves, and a bunch of people came up to the stage to tip the girls dancing with me. For the finale, the lead girl in the pink, sat me down in a chair and gave me a lap dance. I looked up at one point and caught a glimpse of a dude that looked familiar to me. Once the lights shifted out of my eyes, I got a better glance. It was the guy from the airport! My heart jumped and I tried not to make it obvious that I had stopped paying attention to the girl living in my lap. I got semi erect thinking about me riding him, like she was grinding on me.

I had to do something to get his attention and ran through several scenarios in my head before I got back to the table. My crew was all around me partying, but the only one in the room that mattered and who I saw was, "You can call me, Pen." I wanted to know what his story was. I wanted to see "what's up." I kept stealing subtle glances at him. He was wearing a fitted with the D on the front. He was cute as hell with his big swole self. He had a nice sold thick build that I could see myself cuddled up against. His beard was thick and full and trimmed like he was fresh from the barbershop. I was wondering if he remembered where he knew me from because I was still trying to figure out why now it felt like the airport wasn't the first place I saw him either.

I decided to make a bold move once the waitress asked me if I wanted anything else. I smiled and pulled her in close to tell her to send four bottles of Guinness to Pen's table. I asked her to serve his in a frosty mug and to tell him I said hello. Several minutes later, I watched the waitress deliver the drinks to his booth, seductively honoring my request. His face lit up like a Christmas tree as one of the guys and the girl with him grabbed a brew and gave each other a toast. He looked over at me and nodded his head. I smiled as he stood up motioning for me to join him on the patio. I followed suit excusing myself.

"Where you runnin' off too?" Michael asked, grabbing my arm.

"I'm going to see a man about a condom," I laughed.

"Be quiet, fool," he laughed. "You going to the bathroom?" he asked looking at me with skepticism.

"I'm about to go out on the patio to get some air right quick," I said.

"I'll come with you? You alright?" he asked with concern in his voice. "It was just a lap dance shit shawty, don't trip," he said. He was feeling his liquor.

"No! I'm just going to be a minute. Plus I want to be nosy. I'll be right back," I said escaping before his next question.

I took a breath, straightened out my shirt, and wiped my face to make sure I wasn't shiny. I put on a smile walking past the booth that housed him and his friends. I wasn't nervous like I thought I would be. I was in shock that he was actually here in the same city as me. Did he follow me somehow? Was he here on vacation by chance? Damn he is cute as hell! All these thoughts ran through my mind as I walked up to him and posted with strong confidence. He was holding on to his mug, smiled and opened the door to let me enter first. I tugged my shirt real quick, so my booty wasn't all the way out.

The patio was heated and covered with stools and small round tables. It was dimly lit and decorated with live trees and party lights. I walked over to the railing and turned to face him. He smiled again showing me a perfect set of pretty white teeth. We had the patio to ourselves. His lips looked gooder than a mug as he licked his tongue out to catch a drop that dripped down from a drink he took.

"You making me nervous man," he joked, wiping his mouth. "Thank you for the round of beer. How'd you know this was my brew of choice?" He kept that smile going reeling me in. I was trying to resist; not even sure what the hell I was doing.

"You're welcome. You look like the Guinness type," I smiled. He started cheesing and turned away nodding. I noticed his tattoos peeking through the collar of his shirt with a smooth sheen in contrast to his beautiful dark skin.

"That's a hell of a guess. You get some points for that," he chuckled.

"I'm glad to hear that because I thought it would help jog your memory. I can still call you Pen, right?" I smiled. He laughed.

"Well, see that depends?" he asked with a mischievous grin.

"On what?" I smiled ready to play his game. The citrus undertone in his cologne triggered private thoughts of us in my head. He smelled so good.

"You leavin' with me. You gon' tell your friends, you cool with that?" he asked. I was geeked up and maybe I wasn't thinking clearly as I answered.

"I'm cool with that."

"Bet," he smiled.

"If! You cool with telling me your real name? I mean you raised the stakes," I said leaning back against the beam with my hands in my pockets. I gave him a sexy smile awaiting his reply.

"Upendo Reign. I can show you the meaning behind it, but you gotta come with me," he said placing the mug down. He walked up on me gripping my body. "Happy Birthday," he said moving in to kiss me. I stopped him just as we were about to make contact.

"I'm going to go let my big bro know what's up. Upendo," I said giving him a smile.

"Right answer," he smiled rubbing my forearm.

He followed closely behind me as we proceeded to our respective parties to let them know we were about to dip. Where too? I don't know. To do what exactly? I haven't the foggiest. I was either living in the moment or putting my best slut forward...

THREE LITTLE LETTERS

The moment you know what happens to someone, you gotta think about it. Sometimes, it gives you a better understanding about how they operate. Maybe who they are or pretend to be. The way they move through life. The choices they make. The things they let go and leave behind. Especially when there's a connection. But it's funny how one thing in common effects each person differently. You don't think about that shit until they tell you how the world looks from the shoes tied to their feet. What they go through in the quiet times. The doubts and inadequacies we feel we have to fix because of the circumstances handed to us. Your thoughts are not everyone else's. And our thoughts damn sure ain't God's. I think stuff that makes sense to Him won't make sense to us until we have the courage to ask the actual questions that need to be asked.

So no matter how much galavantin' I do through the weeknights, I make it a point to make it to the church house on Sunday. Sometimes I make the good ol' hour of power at 8am or the mid-morning service with everybody else. No matter what city I'm in, or what state of mind I'm in. Church is always on my to-do list. My momma made it a mandatory thang growing up. She used to say, I don't care what you do with your time Friday and Saturday, you carrying your tail to the temple on Sunday to give the good Lawd his time. When I got my license I used to drive her to church when my dad would work nights and couldn't go with us. He didn't go all the time, and Momma never nagged him about it. But when he did go with us, she would sing and hum even sweeter in the midst of her Sunday morning routine.

I don't go out of necessity no more. I go for me. And these days, I find myself singing along to the same praise songs she used to listen to back in the day while I'm getting myself ready. I was the only one coming back to Jason's after the party. He ended up leaving with some strange guy that none of us seen before. He was a'ight looking. I'd say he's Jason's typical type. It's something about him that got my "spidey" senses tingling though. I didn't trip with the big brother grip since it was his birthday and all. Just told him to be careful and wrap it up if he was going to pound town. He texted me to let me know he was cool, so that set my mind at ease, even though I was still a little worried.

Corey and I have been getting more serious these days and after a little coaxing these past few weekends, I convinced him to change his mind about going to church with me. He had my truck and drove over to Jason's so we could ride together. We were going to meet up with the crew for brunch afterwards and I planned to officially introduce him to Corey. I had a special prayer I was going to lay on the alter seeing as the first time Jason saw him, I was all up in them guts. I always wanted to have a boo to go to church with and share my love for God. Corey was still unsure about going and I let him know it wasn't no pressure on my part. Hopefully he would find the same peace and joy that I did and be attending with me on more than this one occasion...

"Follow me upstairs baby so I can finish getting dressed," I said rushing down to let him in the house. I kissed him two or three times and turned running up the steps. He tipped quietly behind me.

"Mike Mike, can I ask you a question?"

"You ain't got to ask that," I smirked.

"What does God look like to you now that you've lived with the virus for this long?" Corey asked me this question while I was puttin' the finishing touches on a bowtie I had finished ironing. I felt good in spite of my slight hangover from the night before.

"God is still God, baby. What you mean?" I asked popping my dose of stay in the world pills. I took a guzzle of water and put my medicine box back in my bag slinging my tie around my neck.

"Well, Mike Mike, you can't possibly believe the same way you once did. Okay, let me say it like this, did you believe in God more or less after you got it?" he asked.

"That's a...damn." I said as I realized I missed a step. I stopped tying my tie for a second to look at him. I never thought about when I got it. "I still believe in God. I grew up in the church. Now, if you asking if I think this is punishment for the things I do with men? Hell naw?" I finished what I was doing and turned to look at him. He was trying to smile as he leaned up against the wall.

"Come here," I said grabbing him by the hands. We went downstairs and sat in the living room. "Where is this coming from? You a'ight?" I smiled trying to get him to look me in the eye.

"I ain't been to church since I found out. It's bad enough they judge us for having no choice being gay. But do you ever think they're right?" he asked.

"Naw. Baby, nooo. And my church ain't judgy, or no shit...or nothing like that. We have all come short of the glory. At least that's what I been taught," I said smiling. I gave him a wink.

"I hear all that. But I'm talking about God. Do you think he did this to us on purpose? Because of what the Bible says about us. I mean I see you take your pills like its nothing. Do you struggle with that? Have you ever thought that's God's way of throwing this sin up in our face every single day. Each time we gotta swallow that poison and try to put on a brave face for people that look at you like you are beneath them. That doesn't bother you?" he asked as his eyes started misting. His hands were trembling.

THREE LITTLE LETTERS

"Baby, no I don't look at it like that. And you shouldn't either. The only thang you can do is live your life. God don't love us any less for making the decisions we make day to day like any other person. God ain't a man, but we are God just with little g's. I believe in God and what I know God to be for myself. Not what people say. Okay, check dis out. Do you think cancer is a punishment? Or hell the common cold? You think those illnesses are punishment?" I asked.

"It's not the same thing," Corey said dabbing at his eye.

"Why come it ain't? You are who you are. And no virus is going to change the man God say you are."

"The condom broke and that's how I got it. I did everything I knew in my power to safeguard my sexual encounters and I still got this thing I can't get rid of. I felt like it was God telling me, I told you so! Maybe even they told you so, too. And it pisses me off sometimes," Corey said looking at me with serious intent.

"Corey, I was born with it. My momma was raped by some white man who gave her the virus. So am I or was I being punished for my sexuality without knowing what sexuality was as a fetus. I mean, I never thought I was wrong. Momma never condemned me for it. So I didn't feel like I needed to condemn me or let no one else do it either. I learned that fate has nothing to do with faith." I confided hoping that would help.

"Really?" he said searching for me to say more. "That's how it happened to you?" I wiped his face with my hands.

"Yes, that's how it happened to me. Before I knew what the world was, or anything like that. I started life with HIV. Before the measles, before ear infections, before chicken pocks, I was HIV positive. God ain't have nothing to do with me getting HIV, and God ain't have nothing to do with you getting it either. I think it's some shit man did to us. A psychopath took advantage of my momma in her time of need, and some lazy rubber manufacturer messed up the condom you used that night. Either that or the nigga you fucked with picked the wrong size or put a hole in it to sneak and fuck raw. Either way it go baby, that wasn't God. God is love and He made me to love you," I said. Tears started coming down his face.

"I'm sorry," he said as I pulled him up off the couch to give him a strong hug.

"Aww, it's a'ight, shawty. You ain't got nothing to be sorry about. Okay? We can skip service today if you want too. I can catch T.D. Jakes online or something," I said.

"No, we can go. I don't need you to log onto Jesus because of me," he said forcing a smile. I kissed his lips and wiped his tears with my thumbs holding his face in my palms.

"As long as I'm here, I won't let these three letters get the best of you or me. Or anybody else I know. And trust me, God won't either. Okay?" I said kissing him again. He shook his head yes.

"I'm sorry, Mike Mike," Corey said looking away. I loved hearing him call me that.

"Don't be sorry baby," I said catching his gaze again. "Is we going to church or naw?" I asked with a chuckle.

"Yeah. Yeah, we can go. To church," he said with a sigh of relief almost.

"You sure?" I smiled, holding onto him.

"I don't know if I'm sure, but maybe after a Sunday or two with you, I will be." He managed to smile for real this time.

"I'm positive you will, a'ight," I said as he nodded his head. "Go fix your make-up and let's go before Jason get home. I'ought feel like hearing his mouth about a stranger in his house. Plus I want to get a good seat. I ain't never late for Jesus, nah," I said swatting his booty as he rushed off to the bathroom...

THE MORNING AFTER

Even though I did a just in case it goes down birthday prep, my plan was not to give it up to Pen on the first night. He damn sure had the green light so far. There was a level of intrigue that had me captivated. I wanted to know more about him. I was probably doing the most leaving with him the way I did. Neither of us drove that night as we were at the mercy of our friends vehicle wise. Normally this would be a problem for me, but I didn't make it a big deal. It was something romantic about it from a poets point of view. Poetic in a city of violence. Michael was reluctant to let me go. I could see it in his eyes, and he had every right to be a concerned friend, but I was the birthday boy and our crew rule is, we can do what we want to do on our respective birthdays. No questions asked. I was about to live. After what I had been through. I needed to start doing, something.

Upendo Reign. I didn't know about this, brotha. But I wasn't afraid anymore. He melted that away. I was feeling things that I hadn't felt in a while. Horny, maybe? He was a different kind of guy than both Darius and Gary. He was tall like I liked. He has a thick build and this silky beard that covers a smile that truly accents his ruggedly chiseled face. He rocked a smooth baldie and had tribal tattoo's in an intricate sleeve covering his left arm. His eyes were so warm leading to a tender heart he poured into the stories he shares.

So after we left the strip joint, we took the train back into the city to walk the streets and talk and see if we had a vibe. He told me about his mother and how close they were. I'm not sure how it came up, but he wanted her to quit smoking. It was a habit she picked up when things got stressful for her as a single mother raising a man child in the concrete jungle. A vice she tried to quit but eventually settled on a simple cut back. I told him a little about the issues between me and Mama. He offered some good advice in terms of just continuing to be the best example of the "queer" black man I am instead of wasting energy fighting with the image she has in her head of us.

We ended up on the south side to get out of the cold night air by catching 90's night at Club Escape. We danced to all the bangers laughing doing different dances and slow wines in our own little world. We talked about Obama and politics, cars, and the best food spots in the cities we'd been to collectively. I had so much fun. Upendo reminded me of what the newness of getting to know someone looked and felt like. How fun it can be. At some point I got over the idea of holding back and feeling like I was damaged goods or a bad luck charm to a man. I shared a cab ride with the intentions of taking my fast ass back home, but I didn't want the night to end. I took him up on his offer of coming back to his crib for a cozy nightcap...

"Can I tell you a joke about pizza, Petty Officer Williams." He was leaning up against the wall in the dimly lit entry way of the duplex. He had me snug and tight up against him with a locked-on gaze. I was his mission. I thought for a moment about wanting to do more than kiss his lips.

"Nah, it's cheesy," I said bursting into laughter. "Okinawa?" I said knowing exactly where his reference came from. I still wasn't able to place his face, though.

"Oki-fucka-nawa! That's why you so familiar," he said laughing unbuttoning my coat. "Alright. Tell me if you remember this day?"

"Go for it," I answered with intrigue. I felt his hands resting interlocked inside my jeans atop the birthday boy cake.

"I'm sitting in the Medical lab chair on the SeaBee base. A lowly lil' E-3 surrounded by dirt and nasty dirty ass white boys all day. To include the trashy Corpsman we had as our doc. And in walks one of the cutest Black HM3's I had ever seen with our pimply faced doc showing you where the supplies were. Usually, he'd draw our labs, but not that day." He tapped my nose with his index finger. "I didn't mind gettin' stuck by you. You asked if you could tell me a joke? I looked you in the eye. Said yes. You looked down and said, Nah, it's cheesy. I kind of laughed and before I knew what happened you were drawing my blood. You don't know how many times I wanted to punch that white boy through the face for stabbing me with them damn needles." He laughed and scrunched his face together with a grunt.

"Dang. I do remember that day. And here I was thinking you were using a pick-up line." I laughed. "You were my second patient."

"Was I? I couldn't tell. You got skill," Pen said with another one of those smiles.

"Thank you. I was getting my certification so that I could add that to my eval. Your CO was my first patient, and I found him to be one of them corny red neck types," I said as we both laughed. He rubbed the small of my back with his thumbs. I could feel his dick start to wake up.

"Yeah, but he was cool," Pen said laughing as I continued. I pressed my dick tighter against him, so he knew what time it was. It was obvious his print hadn't told the whole story.

"To ease my tension in front of all the people in the room. I told him that joke and stuck his ass when he laughed at the punch line. It worked and he didn't feel a thing." I said grinding on him and elevating my ass up so he could palm some more of it. "So I kept that going to take peoples mind off the stick."

"So do I still call you Petty Officer Williams or is it Mr. Williams?" He asked gesturing for a response. I did a quick recount of everything I may or may not have eaten after we left the house. After a quick bottom assessment and clinch or two, I was happy to report all systems were squeaky clean and ready for erection.

"You can call me Jay, tonight." I smiled as his hands gripped me with more authority. He was brick hard. He looked at me for a moment and then up the stairs. We were still by ourselves. There were no cheers and yells from a noisy crowd posing a threat to our interaction. He caught my gaze again and brought his left hand up to catch my chin. The heat between us was palpable. My dick and his dick were hard as missiles. And something in my gut screamed *Don't stop! Git it! Git it!*

"Well, Jay, you ain't no top are you?" He smiled.

"Let's just say, when we share a condom. You can have the inside, and I'll take the outside." He thought for a second.

"True story. I like that, lil' clever ass. That's sexy," he smiled.

I took control of the momentum and kissed them sexy chocolate lips of his the way I had been wanting to all night. I took off my gloves and stuffed them in my pockets. I kept kissing him softly, rhythmically, passionately, unzipping his coat so I could rub and feel on his firm chest. He was so hard, moving me towards his doorway. He paused removing his keys, with me pinned up against the door. He placed the key in the lock twisting it open.

THE MORNING AFTER

We kissed slowly walking inside removing shoes and coats, then shirts, and socks, and pants, kissing from wall to wall across the creaky wooden floor.

Chest to chest. His big dick anxious to greet mine outside of my underwear soaked in the precum leaking down my shaft. I grabbed his erection still deeply kissing as we made our way into his bedroom. I started to remove his briefs to release him from his birdcage. He did the same growing and grunting a subtle damn getting his first true feel of what my jeans withheld. His girth sandwiched mine between his abs and my abs. He laid me down on the bed and went to light a couple of candles. I removed the blanket on the bed and sat up on my knees admiring his strong chocolate physique. The smell of the cologne he wore was all over my body now. The scent of the oils in his beard blended well with the sexy fragrance. I bit my lip as he pulled out a fresh pack of golden tickets and a black bottle of lube. I grabbed his fitted placing it on my head.

Pen walked over towards me with a remote control and a smile. He hit play and the system pumped some West Coast joints through the house speakers. He reached down and pulled me towards him joining me on the bed in between my thighs. I wrapped my legs around his waist and held on to him while we kissed deep as we could go. Tupac's first verse in 'I'd Rather be Your Nigga' thumped in the background. He began grinding and lapping his way down my body before grappling my ankles together inspecting the site he would soon excavate. His tongue found its way to my ground as his lips scooped and sucked up the flow. I felt like I was on another planet the way he made that junk feel. I held my legs apart seductively placing knees to ears as he cupped my ass in his hands. Burying that tongue in me entertained by all of my sex faces.

I heard him unwrap a condom and prepare himself as my mental readied myself for all he had. *Awesome, I don't have to suck his dick tonight,* I thought to myself making a mental note. *I got you next time Pen, if its good.* He lubed me up with a firm middle finger, positioning himself on top of me kissing me. I rolled him over on his back and straddled him. Teasing him and letting him inch his big ass dick up inside me ring by ring. Getting used to the feel of him. The hardness of him. That thick upward curve of his. The need of another man had me going and clinging to a sexual energy that I hadn't noticed needed to be unleashed until now.

I changed the tempo slowly sliding up and down on his dick with a light rotation taking my time to enjoy my body give way to him. I let out heavy breaths and deep moans while he held my waist. I picked up the pace gripping him beginning to handle that shit like it was always mine. We were in competition with his neighbors upstairs. No hands needed as I let my mind go, my inhibitions were out the window, when I looked him in them eyes and bit my lip smiling.

I went to work on his curve and started rolling my hips to the bass and rhymes, grooving to the music setting the tone for our mattress dance. I had his eyes rolling back and I had them toes curling up too. His dick felt so freaking good. I wasn't ready when he put me in doggy and then on my stomach slow grinding, then beating, then digging, and tearing my ass up. I didn't know what was coming next as we both got caught up in the synergy permeating the room. It was like our bodies were rescuing and repairing one another.

I woke up early the next morning wrapped up in his arms like something he would miss when not there. It was so euphoric I was almost reluctant to leave. I needed to get home, but I didn't want to disturb the quiet rumble he played in my ear. I relaxed closer to him and looked at the snowflakes fall as the opener to the day. I thought about the number of times we got it in last night. I thought about the way it felt when I put him inside my world. I started thinking how stupid it would be to start letting myself catch feeling for this dude. But I couldn't reduce him to just a bust down. Because sex like that ain't just sex. But I had to find a way to make it be like that so I wouldn't get distracted.

I'm fighting the connection with this dude. I feel him in my soul, but I'm not trying to do this love thing right now, but shit he feels so good, and he got some really good dick. Oh my God, I can't do this right now! Or get another dude killed. I panicked thinking back on each time we did it unsure if one out of the three were condom free. I got lifted with him last night too. I never asked him his status, and I know he ain't ask for mine.

I woke him up by pretending to stretch. He pulled me back in his arms and began speaking in my ear...

"Where you going lil' daddy?" He kissed my neck then playfully bit my shoulder.

"I need to get home. I'm supposed to be meeting some friends for brunch today," I said trying to figure out how to ask the question I didn't think to ask.

"Every gay man in America goes to Sunday Brunch. What's the hype?" He chuckled. I laughed thinking maybe I was okay. Maybe I didn't need to ask, he was cool. He would have said something. Right? I thought. We heard the sounds of muffled voices and footsteps coming down the stairs from the outside entryway. Upendo jumped up and ran to peek through the curtains with obvious glee. "I knew it was her!"

"Our audience and competition?" I laughed as he nodded his head yes and jumped back into bed scooping me up again.

"That wasn't no walk of shame kiss." He laughed sucking on my neck with a quick nip. "So what's the hype?"

"It's just another place where we go to talk about the guys we met on Saturday and pretend we actually learned something profound at church," I laughed.

"What guy you gon' talk about today?" he asked releasing me from his embrace. He rolled his beautiful naked body over on his back. I straddled him looking him in the eyes. He rubbed my face.

"Probably the old stud holding the bar down," I said cracking up.

"That girl, man, I was shook when she raised up on me. She was serious about them classics," he said laughing and rubbing his beard.

"BREH! Don't be steppin' on my Reeboks, breh! I just shoe polished dese, breh! A scuffed Reebok ain't sexy, breh!" I said mocking her squeaky voice before we both started laughing.

"You and your smile is sexy as fuck, though. I like you, breh!"

"I like you too," I said not even trying to deny it.

"True story, Jason. I really fuckin' like you," he smiled which made me start blushing and junk. I traced his chest with my fingertips.

"For real? Because you don't know my whole story yet," I said not sure if I should let him in or not.

"Yes, I'm for real, which is why I need to be forthright with you, where I wasn't before." I thought he was either going to tell me he was married or maybe something silly.

THE MORNING AFTER

"What you married or got a boyfriend who is about to come home with you trapping me in the closet?" I said laughing waiting for him to join in.

"No, nothing that deep, but it is deep. And you're actually going to be the first person I tell this too," he said with a serious look on his face. He caressed my side. I got comfortable in his lap and dialed my smile back a little bit.

"Okay, well what is it?" I asked as he closed his eyes and then opened them commanding my gaze.

"Full disclosure. I'm HIV positive..."